THE PERILS OF SHERLOCK HOLMES

— SHORT STORIES —

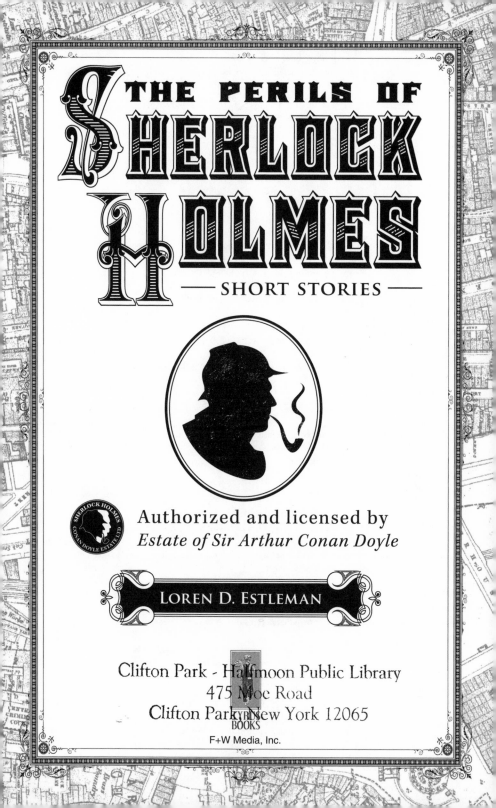

Authorized and licensed by
Estate of Sir Arthur Conan Doyle

LOREN D. ESTLEMAN

BOOKS

F+W Media, Inc.

Published by
TYRUS BOOKS
an imprint of F+W Media, Inc.
10151 Carver Road
Suite 200
Blue Ash, Ohio 45242
www.tyrusbooks.com

ISBN 10: 1-4405-4414-X
ISBN 13: 978-1-4405-4414-9
eISBN 10: 1-4405-4520-0
eISBN 13: 978-1-4405-4520-7

Printed in the United States of America.

10   9   8   7   6   5   4   3   2   1

Library of Congress Cataloging-in-Publication Data

Estleman, Loren D.
 The perils of Sherlock Holmes / Loren D. Estleman.
  p. cm.
 ISBN 978-1-4405-4414-9 (hardcover) – ISBN 1-4405-4414-X (hardcover) – ISBN 978-1-4405-
4520-7 (ebook) – ISBN 1-4405-4520-0 (ebook)
1. Holmes, Sherlock (Fictitious character) 2. Detective and mystery stories, English. 3. Private
investigators–England–Fiction. I. Title.
 PS3555.S84P47 2012
 813'.54–dc23   7ﾌ75
                    2012025207

Grateful acknowledgment to Conan Doyle Estate Ltd. for permission to use the Sherlock Holmes
characters created by Sir Arthur Conan Doyle.

Images © 123rf.com/old-maps.co.uk

*This book is dedicated to the memory of Martin H. Greenberg,
who was every writer's best friend and the patron saint of the short story.
God speed, Marty.*

CONTENTS

CHANNELING HOLMES........................... 9

THE ADVENTURE OF THE ARABIAN
    KNIGHT... 17

THE ADVENTURE OF THE THREE
    GHOSTS.. 39

THE RIDDLE OF THE GOLDEN
    MONKEYS..................................... 65

DR. AND MRS. WATSON AT HOME:
    A COMEDY IN ONE UNNATURAL ACT........ 83

THE ADVENTURE OF THE COUGHING
    DENTIST....................................... 89

THE ADVENTURE OF THE GREATEST
    GIFT... 115

THE DEVIL AND SHERLOCK HOLMES.......... 137

THE SERPENT'S EGG............................. 161

ON THE SIGNIFICANCE OF BOSWELLS......... 185

WAS SHERLOCK HOLMES THE SHADOW?
    (A TRIFLE).................................... 197

SUGGESTED READING........................... 203

ACKNOWLEDGMENTS 208

otwithstanding the hundreds of book-length pastiches in print, only a handful of single-author Sherlock Holmes collections have appeared since Arthur Conan Doyle's death.

All but one of the stories were published in anthologies authorized by the Sir Arthur Conan Doyle literary estate. The final story, "The Serpent's Egg," appears here for the first time.

In addition, three previously published essays, "Channeling Holmes," "On the Significance of Boswells," and "Was Sherlock Holmes The Shadow? (A Trifle)" have been revised and expanded for this book.

The book concludes with a list of Sherlock Holmes–oriented publications recommended by the author.

Loren D. Estleman is the author of nearly seventy novels, including the long-running Amos Walker, private detective, series, *Sherlock Holmes vs. Dracula, or The Adventure of the Sanguinary Count*, and *Dr. Jekyll and Mr. Holmes*. In thirty years, the Sherlock Holmes novels have rarely been out of print.

All the material in *The Perils of Sherlock Holmes* has been approved by the Sir Arthur Conan Doyle literary estate, represented by Jon Lellenberg, a member of the board of directors, and permission has been given the author to use the characters created by Conan Doyle.

CHANNELING HOLMES

t's customary for writers writing about their personal interest in Sherlock Holmes to begin with the details of their first experience of him. I can't, because I can't recall a time when he wasn't known to me on some level.

In all the vast panoply of immortal literary characters, I can think of only four who have entered the dictionary with definitions of their own. To "create a Frankenstein," be called "a real Jekyll and Hyde," or address someone as "Sherlock" requires no explanation, even for an immigrant learning the English language. (Jekyll and Hyde, of course, present the problem of whether to consider them as two characters or one.) Yet Sherlock Holmes stands alone as a pictorial icon as well, and one that crosses all boundaries: class, generation, and geography.

One's image of Frankenstein (or rather of his monster) depends on whether he grew up watching Boris Karloff,

Christopher Lee, or Robert De Niro. *The Strange Case of Dr. Jekyll and Mr. Hyde* has been reprinted and filmed so many times, and imagined by so many different illustrators and actors, that no two people can be selected at random who agree on their appearance. But everyone can identify the eagle-beaked profile in the fore-and-aft cap with the calabash clamped between his teeth.

It doesn't signify that the cap and curved pipe appear only in illustrations, and not in any of the fifty-six short stories and four novels that Sir Arthur Conan Doyle wrote involving Sherlock Holmes. Our image of Christ is wholly the creation of Renaissance painters working sixteen hundred years after the Crucifixion. Neither Mark nor Matthew nor Luke nor John saw need to describe his Lord. The human imagination paints impressions; the retina takes pictures.

So I was aware of Holmes at an early age. Reading would come later, and seeing him onscreen in between. I think it was during my sophomore year in high school that the Detroit CBS affiliate ran a week-long screening of the Universal Sherlock Holmes series on television, introduced by Basil Rathbone, its star. I swindled my parents into letting me stay up late four school nights in succession to watch the films. As has often happened during a movie-loving life (Martin Scorsese's *The Age of Innocence* introduced me to the works of Edith Wharton in my forties), I became infatuated with a character on celluloid, then continued the affair on paper. Bleary-eyed the morning of the fifth day, I stumbled into the school library and checked out *A Study in Scarlet* and *The Sign of Four*.

Sign was a revelation. It was there I learned that Sherlock Holmes occupied his mind with cocaine when not engaged on a case. This was just after the Summer of Love (which I spent painting my parents' vacation cabin in northern Michigan), many years before dope-smoking presidents, heroin-shooting movie stars, and line-snorting junior executives made their appearance; the three-martini lunch was as stimulated as Corporate America ever got. My school system had only recently substituted "Community" for "Agricultural" in its name. There was talk of upperclassmen passing around joints in the parking lot during football games, but I was inclined to dismiss this as urban legend. We had only one hippie, who was stranger to us than the foreign-exchange student from East Pakistan. The prospect of a detective who injected cocaine catapulted me into the world of the noir antihero, and a forbiddingly intoxicating environment for a boy of sixteen.

I should state for the record that entertainment wasn't my sole aim. My dream was to be a cartoonist, and I had made inroads by drawing, stapling together, and selling comic books to my fellow students. A trailer for the film (movies, again) *A Study in Terror*, pitting Holmes against Jack the Ripper, had started me thinking about doing something similar in a comic book, and since I'd recently read Bram Stoker's *Dracula* for the first time, I thought it fitting that these literary contemporaries meet; they were in London at the same time, after all.

Sherlock Holmes Meets Dracula sold out quickly, as one copy ought to, and I hope whoever bought it still has it. It must be worth something by now as the earliest version of my all-time best-selling novel, and I'd like a childhood friend to prosper. The story was facile, not at all canonical either to Stoker or Conan Doyle, but the appropriateness of the match was still with me ten years later, when Nicholas Meyer's *The Seven-Per-Cent Solution* soared up every list of national bestsellers, and I'd shifted my career objectives from graphic arts to writing.

By this time, I was far more familiar with the literary Holmes. In 1976, I'd joined The Arcadia Mixture, Ann Arbor's scion of the national Baker Street Irregulars, and had sold a freelance piece on the group to the local newspaper. To supplement my knowledge, I reread *Dracula*, outlined the plot thoroughly, created a parallel timeline with the Holmes stories as calculated by Sherlockian scholars, and pored over a shelf of material on Victorian England. I began each writing day by reading a Holmes story or a fragment of one of the novels. With the Doylean/Watsonian language patterns fresh in my mind, I wrote:

> *I need hardly consult my notebook for 1890 to recall*
> *that it was in August of that year that my friend Mr.*
> *Sherlock Holmes, with some slight assistance by me, set*
> *out to unravel the single and most terrible bone-chilling*
> *mystery which it has been my privilege to relate.*

Sherlock Holmes vs. Dracula, or The Adventure of the Sanguinary Count was published by Doubleday July 15, 1978; the day that a reviewer for the *New York Times*, writing about someone else's book, said was the absolute worst date to bring out a novel of any kind, as everyone was away on vacation and certainly not inclined to spend one precious moment of his holiday browsing in a bookstore. My book sold 20,000 copies, which is still considered more than respectable for a hardcover book by an unknown author. Paperback rights went to Penguin, which distributed it throughout the English-speaking world. The BBC bought broadcast rights and aired it on radio. It was translated into Swedish, Danish, Spanish, and Dutch.

Penguin published it in a new mass-market edition ten years after the first, and just as it was passing out of print in America, the Book-of-the-Month Club picked it up for trade paperback. Many years later the late Byron Preiss distributed it as both trade paper and mass-market editions under the I-Books imprint. It was optioned twice by Hollywood (which approached Pierce Brosnan and Alexander Godunov for the leads), and was very nearly pirated by another studio until a threat of legal action shut down the production.

In thirty-five years, the book has rarely been out of print. (To put its longevity into perspective, consider that the original price in hardcover was $7.95, less than the average mass-market paperback of today.)

It's more famous than its author—a phenomenon that vexed Conan Doyle in his day, and drove him to the ill-advised decision to murder Holmes in order to prevent his own obscurity. When strangers ask me what I've written—which is a polite way of saying they've never heard of me—I enjoy watching their faces light up when I mention this one title out of more than sixty.

The credit, of course, is not mine. Fans of Holmes and Dracula would populate a good-size country. I'd tapped into both groups. I'm prouder of having pleased the late Dame Jean Doyle Bromet, Sir Arthur's daughter, who acknowledged my respect for the original by exempting me from a temporary ban she'd placed on Holmes pastiches. (Like her father, she'd begun to fear that the character might overshadow his creator.) The board that still represents the author's estate in the United States has extended the compliment by giving me permission to publish the present collection.

My second foray in this expanding subgenre was *Dr. Jekyll and Mr. Holmes*, which I think is the better effort. But iconography aside, Jekyll and Hyde claim only a fraction of Dracula's following. The book has ocasionally been out of print for long intervals, although trade-paper editions were issued by I-Books in 2001 and Titan Books in 2010. Both books appeared between the same covers in a trade paper book published in 1995 by the Quality Paperback Book Club.

I considered a trilogy, but when one snarky critic wrote that "Estleman is no doubt busy writing about Holmes and Fu Manchu," I abandoned my plan for that very pairing; I dislike giving even prescient snipers the opportunity to be smug. Later, Cay Van Ash, a friend and biographer of Sax Rohmer, Fu Manchu's creator, threw the Oriental criminal mastermind into the ring with Holmes in *Ten Years Beyond Baker Street*, ably filling that gap in adventure fiction. (I did manage to smuggle Rohmer into "The Riddle of the Golden Monkeys.")

I keep my hand in, as the reader will see. All but one of the stories in *The Perils of Sherlock Holmes* have appeared in collections edited by Jon Lellenberg, a member of the board of directors of the Sir Arthur Conan Doyle estate, and the late Martin H. Greenberg, with the occasional assistance of Daniel Stashower and Carol Lynn Waugh. This is the first time they've all appeared in one collection. "The Serpent's Egg," intended as the first chapter of a collaborative "round robin" novel that never came off, appears here for the first time in print. It is my belief that *The Perils of Sherlock Holmes* is the first single-author collection of Holmes short stories published since Sir Arthur Conan Doyle's own *The Case-Book of Sherlock Holmes* (although *The Exploits of Sherlock Holmes* may be the exception; presented as a collaboration between Adrian Conan Doyle, Sir Arthur's son, and John Dickson Carr, it may in fact have been written entirely by Carr).

Whenever I'm asked to contribute a Sherlock Holmes story to an anthology, I agree. They always pay royalties, unlike many collections of short fiction (my first submission, a one-act play called *Dr. and Mrs. Watson at Home*, still surprises me with checks a quarter-century after it appeared in *The New Adventures of Sherlock Holmes*), but if that were the only incentive, I would decline. The stories are fun to write, and I appreciate the opportunity to stay in touch with my Watsonian side.

These days, I find it less necessary to bone up by reading the originals, whole sections of which I've committed to memory, the way a lay preacher memorizes the books of the Old and New Testaments. I merely switch gears, from twenty-first century to nineteenth, and from America to England, and I'm off again among the yew hedges, cockney constables, hunting hounds, dinner at Simpson's, and a Crook's Peerage of disgraced family crests. Just as Donald Duck's Uncle Scrooge delights in diving beak-first into his money bin, I dog-paddle and Australian-crawl my way through the recherché vocabulary and dependent clauses of John H. Watson, M.D., with a grin on my face and "God Save the Queen" playing over and over in my head.

I have, I confess, an unfair advantage over some others who try to walk and talk like the Victorians. Not counting Holmes stories, I spend only half my time writing contemporary suspense. The other half I apply to historical westerns.

A non sequitur, you say? You're thinking of the wrong kind of western. In the westerns I enjoy reading and am privileged to write, no one ever says, "Slap leather, ya sidewinder," or drops his *g*'s the way a buffalo sheds hair. Nor did anyone ever speak that way on the frontier. The average sixth-grade-educated pioneer had a firmer grasp of grammar (taught at the end of a hickory stick) than today's average college graduate. His vocabulary was larger, and surviving letters and journals read like—well, Victorian novels. Then as now, ordinary people tended to speak the way they wrote letters; these written records are the closest thing we have to voice recordings. Wyatt Earp and Doc Holliday would no sooner double a negative than wear a flannel shirt to see *Richard III* at the Birdcage Theatre in Tombstone. With this wisdom, once I get caught up in the rhythms of the early Industrial Age, I often feel that I'm channeling Conan Doyle rather than just borrowing his style.

It is possible, however, to try to out-Doyle Doyle, and err in the attempt. Upon fresh review, these stories as written struck me as unnecessarily wordy even by his standards. I've tightened and trimmed the language—extensively, in some cases—and present them in a different form from the way they appeared the first time. I consider the changes an improvement; not over the original material in the Canon, but over my own early efforts to pay it tribute.

The canonical style, perhaps, is dated, although it never seems so when the main characters are trading witticisms, or when one of them is drawing a bead on the enemy with his revolver while the other pilots a steam launch at full throttle down the racing Thames River. The aftereffect is indelible. Every decade of the twentieth century produced a motion picture about Sherlock Holmes, beginning in 1900. The present century has continued that tradition, most recently with two vivid reimaginings of the legend through the acting talents of Robert Downey, Jr., and Jude Law. Both films were blockbusters at the box office.

Sherlock Holmes is forever green, and startlingly cutting-edge to those who discover him for the first time. But for him and the characters of Charles Dickens, we might dismiss the late colonial British Empire as a stagnant pool of repressed passion, pious hypocrisy, and the right fork for the right course. Through Conan Doyle's gimlet eye and razor nib, we know that it was a time of stupendous scientific achievement, sweeping social change, artistic beauty, and crime to raise the hackles on the neck of a gangsta rapper. It was the time of Charles Darwin, Sigmund Freud, Susan B. Anthony, Vincent Van Gogh, Kaiser Wilhelm II, drug addiction, civil rights demonstrations, labor unrest, and weapons of mass destruction. It was the time of Victoria Regina, Otto von Bismarck, and Grigori Rasputin. It was the time of Sherlock Holmes.

Loren D. Estleman

Whitmore Lake, Michigan

THE ADVENTURE OF THE ARABIAN KNIGHT

"Stand aside, Holmes!" said I, gripping my stick in the defensive position familiar to my service in India and Afghanistan. "Here is a proper cut-throat."

Sherlock Holmes and I were returning from a constitutional which I as his physician had prescribed. For a fortnight, my friend and fellow-lodger had not ventured outside our smoke-filled digs, even to breathe the comparatively less sinister air of greater London, and I feared more than usually for his health.

His confinement comprised an investigation into the mysterious death of Edmond Warworthy, Bart., whose solution Holmes eventually discovered in an entry made some thirty years previously in his journals. These ran to fifty-six volumes dated between 1 January 1832 and 11 August 1888, the day upon which Sir Edmond died.

Our evening out was a balmy one in early September. A trade wind had extinguished the noxious yellow fog that is so typical of autumn in our metropolis, and a sunset of staggering beauty was in full cry over Middlesex, painting the blackest chimneys the colour of claret. However, it's a fair wind that blows nobody bad; for a pleasant climate and creeping shadows provide a hunting ground for two-legged predators in search of complacent strollers with fat purses. Therefore I was alert when a fellow shamming sleep stirred suddenly in the darkness beyond the fanlight of our Baker Street home, and issued the warning recorded above.

In appearance he was of a type not uncommon in that cosmo-politan city: swarthy and bearded, dark as hickory, and swathed in the robes and hooded mantel, called a *burnoose*, which are associated with the Muslims of the Near East. Huddled as he'd been in this voluminous raiment, he might have been taken for a bundle of discarded bedclothes but for the way the whites of his eyes glistened as we approached. When he moved, I prepared to smite him before he could produce a razor-edged dirk and demand our valuables in return for our lives.

Holmes seized my wrist in his iron grip. "Calm yourself, old fellow. This may be a client."

"A client for the jailkeeper in Bow Street, you mean." I held my ground.

"You, there, *Haji*! Kindly oblige a pair of infidels and join us in the light."

For the space of thirty seconds the man in the shadows did not stir, although he continued to watch us like some beast on the edge of a campfire. Then, slowly and with queer dignity, he arose with a rustle and stepped into full view.

I tightened my hold on my trusty Penang Lawyer; for the man was a particularly wicked-looking specimen of Arab. Standing slightly above the medium height, he wore a coal-black beard only a shade darker than his burnished flesh, against which those startling eye-whites shone like scaled pearls, their nut-coloured irises glaring balefully. As if to put the fine point on his devilish countenance, the brigand displayed a vicious scar on either cheek, sunken with age and puckered at the edges, the less noticeable of the pair fully as long as a man's hand is wide. The obvious conclusion, that his face had been transfixed by some savage blade, made me shudder, as if I had witnessed the event at firsthand.

The silken sash he had tied about his waist, red once but now faded like the scars, suggested the ideal girdle for a weapon—not now in evidence, but quite likely concealed somewhere upon his person. I daresay that in that sprawling city of four millions, there was not one who could inspire greater dread.

"A hundred thousand pardons, *effendim*. These ancient eyes are no longer what once they were. The low cur who owns them could not be certain he was in the presence of the great *sahib* detective until he was near enough to smell the breath of the camel."

This fulsome speech, delivered in faultless English, was heavy with the guttural but not unmusical accent of the deserts and oases of popular romance. Of his age, at least, he spoke the truth. The folds and creases in his leathery hide were at the lowest estimate sixty years in the creation. I thought it probable the vain old fellow dyed his whiskers with lampblack.

"I am Sherlock Holmes—in the event there is more than one great *sahib* detective living on this street. This is Dr. Watson, upon whose discretion you may rely as surely as the Bank of England. Whom have I the honour of addressing?"

The fellow bowed whilst performing the pretty *salaam* gesture with his right hand. "Most certainly, respected one, the honour belongs to me. I am called Sheik Abdullah."

"Sheik, if you will allow me the impertinence." Holmes extended a hand and, to my surprise, grasped the Arab's chin and gently turned his face to this side and that, exposing each of the man's scars to the light. "The left is the more pronounced. Would you concur, Doctor, that this is the exit wound?"

"I would. Most tissue damage occurs on the way out."

"Torn palate, Sheik?"

"Yes, *effendim*. And four back teeth for Allah."

"The entry is as clean as an incision. The projectile, then, passed through on the instant, which is seldom the case with anything as long as a conventional spear or as clumsy as a sword or sabre. A javelin, perhaps. Somali?"

"Wonderful, respected sir! I was chief of bearers on safari. Savages attacked us for our goods. Through the grace of the Prophet, blessings and peace be upon him, I fought my way to safety. Alas, others were not so favoured."

The oily obsequiousness of this response made me distrust the stranger all the more, for I had seen surprise, admiration, and suspicion succeed one another in his eyes as Holmes deduced the details of his injury. I found myself wondering if he was not himself the savage behind the attack he spoke of, injured by an accomplice in the heat of action.

"In any case, the affair is years in the past," said Holmes. "The wounds are long healed. It can hardly be the reason for your visit."

"It is not. I have come to consult you upon a matter of grave importance."

"Then let us continue this conversation upstairs. A London street is not the marketplace in Cairo."

"Is it wise, Holmes?" I could not help whispering. "We know nothing of this fellow's reputation."

Grim amusement stirred my friend's spare features. "I might venture to say that were we to know very much more, we would think it even less wise."

With this cryptic remark, he led the way up the well-trodden steps to the cluttered sitting-room whence so many adventures had been launched.

Wordlessly, and with (it seemed to me) a disregard for invitation that ran counter to the humility he sought to express, Sheik Abdullah embarked upon a self-guided tour of the many curious items which were placed carelessly upon exhibit in our homely parlour. His interest in certain things at the expense of others was odd. The Danish dagger that had featured prominently in the Blackwell murder case received only cursory attention, whilst the shabby Persian slipper where Holmes kept his coarse tobacco became an object of some five minutes' close scrutiny. He studied the weave of the hanging basket chair at length, but ignored completely the Borgia ring, for which Holmes had declined a princely offer from the British Museum. Throughout, the detective retained his bemused expression. He suggested a libation. A request for plain water followed.

Our singular guest accepted the glass with effusive gratitude, then went through the elaborate ritual of thanks to the powers of Mohammedism before imbibing. Holmes watched, evidently appreciating the performance.

"Now that you've partaken of our hospitality, Sir Richard, perhaps you will provide an explanation for this show of false colours."

The man in Arabian garb choked, coughed, and lowered the glass, using the loose sleeve of his robe to sponge the drops from his beard. He stared at Holmes. Then his face broke into a sinister smile.

"I see that I am not misled as to your abilities," said he, in a deep voice in which there was now no trace of the Orient. "Pray, tell me where I betrayed myself. In another time and place, the answer may save my life."

"I suspected the truth when I examined your scars. They are more famous than you realise, having spent so much time in the far reaches of Empire and beyond. When I accurately assigned them to a Somali javelin and saw your reaction, I was emboldened further, but withheld certainty until you committed the blunder of accepting and drinking from a vessel with your left hand. No Muslim worthy of his faith would do that."

"Blast!" He glared at the offending hand. "I've been away too long from the Koran. I should have known, when my girdle refused to tie in the old place, that I would be rusty as well as fat. Because I no longer trust the public journals, I assumed your press notices were exaggerations. I beg you to accept the apologies of a retired officer, if not precisely a gentleman."

Impatient and disgruntled, I interposed myself. "I confess I'm at sea, Holmes. What is the name of this fellow, of whose famous scars I was ignorant only moments ago?"

"Really, Watson, it amazes me when fellow members of a guild fail to recognise one another. An old adventurer-journalist such as yourself must be aware of Captain Sir Richard Francis Burton, author of *The Arabian Nights* and discoverer of the source of the River Nile."

"Flattering, but inaccurate upon both counts," protested the other. "The Nile is John Speke's, may his troubled soul find rest, and I merely translated the text of the thousand-nights-and-a-night: The authors are dust these seven hundred years. I shall admit to Lake Tanganyika, and two volumes chronicling my experiences during a pilgrimage to Mecca, among other trifles. My disguise upon that occasion was superior, or I should not be here to boast of it."

As he spoke, our guest removed his hood, exposing gray hair cropped close to his skull and a band of unstained skin at the hairline. It was a remarkable head, with advanced frontal development, fierce brows, and those unique scars, which were even more pronounced without the distraction of a disguise.

"Great Scott!" I exclaimed. "I've followed each installment of the *Nights* as it has appeared. Astounding." I grasped the hand he'd extended, only to break the grip when a fresh and disturbing association presented itself. "But, did you not translate also—" I left off, blushing to pronounce the disreputable title.

"The *Kama Sutra*. I may as well own to that as well. It cost me a club membership."

"There are no forbidden frontiers to an explorer," Holmes said. "Now, Sir Richard, there is the siphon, and there the basket chair you admired. Make free with both and tell us the reason for your fancy dress."

Burton declined the whisky, explaining that as long as he wore Muslim garments he would not blaspheme the faith, but curled himself into the chair in the same extra-Occidental fashion that my friend was wont to adopt. The old adventurer was exceptionally supple for a man nearing his threescore and ten.

"You will find, Holmes, as you continue to acquire notoriety, that people do not always conduct themselves in your presence as they would under most circumstances. It's an intolerable nuisance, as it slows the process of character judgement. An incognito visit seemed the best way to save time. As things turned out, I was right. You are indeed the man for the job I have in mind."

Holmes, seated in his favourite armchair, lit his pipe and said nothing. I noted with interest that he had selected the old black clay he preferred when in a contemplative humour.

Burton continued. "I am at present only a temporary resident of London. My leave expires next month, when I return to my post at the British Consulate in Trieste. Meanwhile I am engaged in a number of projects, one of which is the translation of documents which came into my hands in 1860, when I was on the Ivory Coast. That is to say, I *was* so engaged, until four weeks ago; but I shall come to that. How much do you know, Holmes, about ancient culture in Egypt?"

"Rather less than I do about modern criminal enterprise in Brixton. Do the subjects intersect?"

"Possibly, although I'm uncertain about Brixton. The document is a transcription in Second Century Aramaic from a hieroglyphic scroll that was burned in the great fire that consumed Alexandria. I translated just enough of it into English to form the conclusion that it provides explicit directions to the tomb of a Pharaoh who ruled during the Eighteenth Dynasty."

At this point, Holmes, to my chagrin and Burton's astonishment, yawned.

"Forgive me, Sir Richard, but unless the Pharaoh was done to death I confess little interest in the affair thus far. The good doctor can enlighten you upon the futility of instructing me in anything not related to the science of deduction."

"Just so," said our guest; but it was plain he regretted denying himself the reinforcement of strong spirits. "As to the nature of the king's demise, I am without illumination. He expired before his twentieth year, but beyond that I know nothing save that he was a son of Akhenaton, the Sun King. The boy's name was Tutankhamen—King Tut, if you find the diminutive less challenging to pronounce."

"They ring no bells, either of them."

"Nor should they. They do not appear on any of the royal lists which have come down to us. For that matter, the extent to which he was stricken from history emboldens me to hope that his burial vault is undefiled. It will come as no surprise to you that grave-robbing was not invented by Burke and Hare. To date, archaeologists digging in the Valley of the Kings have failed to unearth a single tomb that was not stripped of its treasures centuries before Christ. Mummies, yes. Pottery, certainly. Ancient writings invaluable to historians. But not one scrap of the gold and precious gems that were buried with the monarchs to comfort them in the Hereafter."

"Perhaps they weren't there to begin with. Pilfering servants were not invented in our age either."

"I reject the premise. They could not *all* have been criminals."

The detective's lids drooped further—a sure sign that his interest was awakened at last. "Pray continue. But please confine your narrative to the present century. What has become of the document?"

"I knew you would surmise it was missing. No other circumstance would have driven me to leave off the task before it was complete. It was stolen, Holmes; spirited away by my assistant while I was out, under my wife's very nose. I am as certain that James Patterson is the thief as I am that polygamy is the instinctive law of nature."

The name of the man he suspected shocked me so deeply that I overlooked his inflammatory last phrase. "Not the son of Colonel Henry Patterson!"

"The same, Doctor. No acorn ever rolled farther from the oak than the offspring of the hero of Roarke's Drift. More fool I, knowing the little bounder's reputation; but mine is scarcely better, and I thought if some stalwart had lent me a hand up when it counted, I might have found a better billet in my decrepitude than a third-rate consulate in the Adriatic. I've paid dearly for my charity. The day after tomorrow marks a month since he walked out on me, with King Tut under his coat."

With the economy of language typical of his writing style, our prospective client described those events which had brought him to our door.

Immediately upon renting the house he shared with his wife, Isabel, Burton had unpacked a trunk he'd kept in storage nearly thirty years, containing papers he'd collected and almost forgotten. The importance of the Tutankhamen manuscript was instantly apparent, and he'd engaged young Patterson to perform errands which would otherwise distract him from his work. Colonel Patterson had disinherited his son upon learning that he'd stolen from him to repay gambling debts, then gotten himself barred from every club in London as a card and billiards cheat. On evidence supplied by his father, James had spent a month in Reading Gaol for petty theft. When he came to Burton with his tale of woe, he was living in Spitalfields with a woman of unsavoury reputation. A man of less than sterling credits himself— Burton's outspoken nature and boundless curiosity about matters best left unexamined preceded him everywhere he went in society—the explorer agreed to take young Patterson on in consideration for room and board and a small wage.

Straight away, Burton realised he'd accepted one challenge too many. Daily the fellow vanished before his work was done, stayed out all night, and the next day could not be roused to begin his duties until late afternoon, whereupon the cycle would repeat itself.

"I had a brief period of hope," said our guest, "when Patterson bought a Kodak camera out of his first week's pay. I thought he was showing an interest in something constructive. However, the novelty of the purchase soon faded. The contraption languished on a shelf in my study while he continued his dissolute course."

One day, Burton returned from the reading room of the British Museum to be told by Lady Isabel that his assistant had given notice and left. An inspection revealed that the Egyptian document was missing. Burton interrogated his wife, who swore that Patterson had come from the study empty-handed, gone up to his room to pack his meagre belongings, and gone out carrying only the worn portmanteau he had when he'd arrived.

She said she'd seen the papers spread out on the desk only a quarter-hour before. Moreover, she'd spent the intervening time writing letters in the little anteroom that separated the study from the stairs, with a view of both. Had he returned to the room, she could not have failed to see him.

"Is the manuscript fairly compact?" asked Holmes at this point in the narrative.

"Anything but. With my notes, which vanished along with it, it was as thick as a city directory. The original parchment is brittle and leaves a trail of brown flakes whenever it's moved."

"Then it's unlikely he carried it out beneath his coat, as you indicated."

"Impossible. That was just a figure of speech."

"Is there a possibility he sneaked back in later? Or that some anonymous thief gained entry between the time Patterson departed and you arrived?"

"There is not. Isabel was in the anteroom the entire time. There is no other entrance to the study except the window, which has been nailed shut since we moved in."

"Have you been in contact with Patterson?"

"As I suspected, he returned directly to the woman in Spitalfields. When I confronted him there, he did not take the trouble to deny the theft. A police search of his quarters failed to uncover the papers, and no amount of threats on my part would persuade him to confess what he had done with them."

"Did you try bribery?"

"Against all my principles, yes. He laughed at me. Ten years ago, I'd have struck the blighter, but my wife has had a domesticating influence. He has me over a barrel, Holmes. The authorities won't jail him without evidence. The insolent creature as much as challenged me to take action. I'd call him out, Isabel or no Isabel, but killing him on the field of honour would not bring back the directions to Tut's tomb." Impotent rage coloured the old knight's features through the artificial pigment.

"Do you think he intends to loot the tomb himself?"

"Hardly. He is not an archaeologist, and the work is heartbreaking even when one has the wherewithal to finance an expedition. He is as lazy as Ludlam's dog and as poor as a leper. His only hope for profit would be to sell the manuscript, but since I've alerted the Royal Geographical Society to that possibility, his only recourse would be to ransom it back to me, for considerably more than I offered the first time. But four weeks have passed, and he has made no attempt to get in touch. Isabel suggested I consult you."

"You have had him watched, no doubt."

"He can't take a step in any direction without being observed by private enquiry agents. The farthest he's travelled is to the corner post office and back. The agents' fees are ruinous, and I am a poor man. The situation cannot continue. The key to the greatest historical find in a generation lies in the hands of a common thief. You are my court of last resort."

"I think of having a placard lettered to that effect." Holmes pulled at his pipe. "I should like to visit your study, if you will have me."

"Certainly, although I fail to see what the visit will achieve. My search was thorough, and the layout is as I described."

"I do not think otherwise. However, as you well know, the source of the Nile remained invisible to those who lived next to it for ten thousand years. Identifying it required a stranger. Watson, be a good fellow and hail us a cab. Tutankhamen awaits."

A brief ride in a four-wheeler deposited us three before an unprepossessing house in Westminster, where Sir Richard presented us to his wife. I found her to be a woman of serene dignity, at whose throat reposed a gold crucifix, in the heart of Protestant England. An adventurer, she, every bit as fearless as her husband, who had penetrated the African interior, Mecca, India, and the Country of the Saints in Utah Territory. She greeted us graciously.

"I hope, Mr. Holmes, you can help Richard locate his pagan shrine. It has the virtue at least of being less dubious than some of his other projects."

"Isabel still entertains the hope of civilising her barbarian," confided our host.

"Would that Jimmy Patterson had absconded with *The Perfumed Garden*." With this Parthian shot—delivered, it seemed to me, without a trace of irony—she left us to our exploration.

Burton's private study was an exhibition hall of Orientalia; the exotic fixtures in our own digs were conventional by comparison. Beaded curtains, scimitars, an Indian hookah, blowguns of various lengths, and at least one shrunken head were interspersed among no fewer than five writing-desks. Sir Richard, reappearing after a brief absence in a proper European turnout of shirt, shoes, waistcoat, and trousers, with most of the stain scrubbed from his skin, informed us that each cluttered desk contained papers related to a different literary enterprise.

"It used to be ten," he added; "but the diplomatic service has gelded the stallion."

Holmes made no response, engaged as he was in his examination of the room. His intense grey eyes scanned the books and *objets d'art* on the shelves, peered inside the kneeholes of desks, and passed without scholarly interest across scattered sheets containing dense notations in

Burton's nervous hand. His hands remained in his pockets until he came to the hearth, where he prodded the smoking ashes of a recent fire with a poker that had begun life as a Sepoy lance.

Holmes replaced the weapon in its holder, then directed his gaze to the leopardskin rug in front of the grate. For several moments he remained in a crouch with his hands spread on his thighs, moving only his eyes. Suddenly he threw himself to the floor, combed his fingers through the short coarse fur, and came to his feet holding something between his forefinger and thumb. With his other hand he fished out his pocket lens to study it more closely. He asked how often there was a fire in the room.

"Every day, even in summer," came the reply. "All those years in the tropics have ruined me for the English climate."

"Tell me, Sir Richard, if you recognise this."

Burton accepted the tiny object, smaller than a child's fingernail. He borrowed the lens, through which he scrutinised it for a few seconds only.

"Parchment, without a doubt, and ancient." He paled. "Good Lord, Holmes! You can't suppose—"

"I never suppose. I only propose. The document left this room by way of the chimney, there to mingle with the rest of the soot coating the most populous city in the world."

"If he burned it, the man is a vandal, which is worse than a thief, and a madman besides. He has acted entirely without purpose, depriving posterity of the way to the riddle of Tutankhamen's burial place. Now it will never be found."

"Let us not be pessimistic. Where there is no reason, deductive reasoning is futile, and I am not prepared to surrender the point. Your vandal theory does not cover the second disappearance which has taken place."

"There is nothing else missing."

"Where, then, is the Kodak camera you said young Patterson abandoned to a shelf in the study?"

The explorer directed his gaze towards a cabinet containing books and exotic bric-a-brac. There was a space between objects.

"I haven't given the bloody thing a thought for weeks. I'm certain it isn't in his old quarters, either. I searched there as well. But certainly Isabel would have seen him carrying it out."

"Possibly not. Apart from its simplicity, the Kodak's chief advantage is portability. He could indeed have hidden it under his coat, apropos your suggestion, however facetious it was intended. The answer that occurs first is often the best."

"But if he photographed the papers, why haven't I received a ransom demand? I'm convinced he's approached no one else."

"For the answer to that, we must wait for morning," said Holmes. "Will your purse enable you to maintain your watch upon him one more night?"

"Just that. I fail to see—"

"Failure to see is the driving force behind exploration. If the fellow attempts to fly tonight, he will have King Tut on his person, and presently you will have him upon yours. Tomorrow, or the next day at the very latest, the Pharaoh will be comfortably ensconced in Westminster. Should it be the next day, Dr. Watson and I shall stand the watch through tomorrow night. By then, one month will have passed since the deed was done, a wizard measure of time. My faith in the efficiency of our government institutions encourages me to expect success."

My friend's cheerful certainty had an effect upon the chronic cynicism of our host, whose ferociousness of feature had abated to some degree. "I shall be in your debt, quite literally. It goes without saying that history will as well."

"History can look to its own account. Yours, Sir Richard, will be discharged if we can prevail upon you to put us up tonight at least. Should Patterson take flight, it's best we learn of the fact simultaneously with you. Action must be taken in concert and at once."

Burton accepted Holmes's terms without hesitation. His major-domo, a Mameluke whose British livery did not subtract from his ferocious countenance, was sent round to our quarters with a note to Mrs. Hudson to pack two overnight cases. By the time he returned, we had dined with Sir Richard and his lady, on curried lamb such as I hadn't tasted since my Indian service, paradoxically prepared by their stoic Scottish cook, and been shown to our room.

It contained two camp beds and various items of arcania which had spilled into it from the master's overladen study. A stuffed mongoose perched on a shelf above my bed, feeding upon a lifelike cobra. That night I dreamt of Calcutta.

Our game had not flown by morning, when Holmes with some difficulty persuaded Burton to stay home rather than accompany us upon our mission.

"Your illustrious scars, and Patterson's familiarity, would put the odds overmuch in his favour. Compose your soul in patience this one time. I assure you the game will prove worthy of the candle."

We donned our simplest garb and alighted from the hansom several squares ahead of our destination. It was a neighbourhood of day-laborers, common loafers, and strangers to prosperity, for whom any unfamiliar visitor who did not arrive by shank's mare or the Underground was suspect.

Holmes, armed with Patterson's description, enquired at the post office on his street, and satisfied himself that our quarry had not been in yet that day. Thereupon we took up our vigil outside the entrance.

There, a group of unfortunates in motley attire crouched glumly on the steps and pavement, hoping to earn a shilling helping the odd customer carry his or her parcels. Upon Holmes's advice, I ignored the black looks we received from our supposed rivals, whilst fingering the revolver in my coat pocket. There were evil faces in that crew, some of whom (I had no doubt) were described in detail in police bulletins posted inside the building.

The day wore on. People of every description, although few thriving in appearance, came and went; fewer still succumbing to our companions' ministrations to relieve them of their burdens upon exiting. Lady Isabel had provided us with cold mutton sandwiches, which we unwrapped at mid-day, and earned some grudging approval from the others when we shared them with those who had not brought along provisions.

Throughout our surveillance, we did not converse beyond the necessary. Curious as I was to learn what we were about, experience had taught me the folly of trying to draw Holmes out on the details of his plans.

Towards late afternoon, a catch in Holmes's breath aroused me from the stupefaction of boredom. His hand closed firmly upon my near wrist. I noted then a youngish man approaching.

He was in need of a haircut and wore a shabby overcoat, but his bearing betrayed breeding. His hair colouring and blue eyes, shot through at that early hour with the ensanguination of strong drink, matched the description Burton had given us of James Patterson, the disinherited son of one of the heroes of Roarke's Drift.

I grasped the handle of my pistol, but was prevented from drawing it out by a quick squeeze of Holmes's hand. Thus we stood unmoving as Burton's late assistant climbed the steps and entered the post office.

Leaning close, Holmes whispered in my ear.

"If he should emerge carrying a parcel, we shall follow him until we're clear of these other fellows. He may have friends among them. Be prepared, upon my signal, to step in close and press your revolver against his ribs. Discreetly, I beseech you; a day at the Assizes to answer a charge of robbery by a passing patrolman may undo a lifetime of respectable behaviour."

An eternity seemed to pass before Patterson reappeared. In truth it was not quite five minutes. He sauntered down the steps, considerably lighter on his heels than he had seemed on the way up. Beneath his right arm, clutched as tightly as if it contained the treasure of the Tower, rode a brown paper–wrapped parcel no larger than an officer's toilet kit.

As directed, I fell in beside Holmes and we trailed the young man at a distance of fifty yards until we were well quit of the crowd outside the post office. Then we picked up our pace, and an instant before the sound of our approaching footsteps must alert Patterson to our presence, Holmes cried, "Now, Watson! Sharp!"

I stepped in quickly, thrusting my weapon's muzzle through the material of my coat pocket against Patterson's side, just as he turned. He seemed to recognise the feel of the tempered steel, for he tensed. At that same instant, the detective circled round in front of him. His eyes were bright.

"Your game is done, Patterson! My friend is no stranger to the hazardous life, and will not hesitate to fire if you offer him no choice. The parcel, if you please." He held out a hand.

The young man wet his lips noisily. "Is it a hold-up, then?" asked he, loudly.

"Were I you, I would not seek to summon police help, however clumsily. It would be the word of a disgraced son against a knight of the realm." Holmes's tone was withering in its contempt.

The tension went out of Patterson like wind from a torn sail. He surrendered the parcel.

Instinctively I stepped back a pace, widening my field of fire, whilst Holmes tore away the coarse brown paper. Within seconds he had exposed a box covered in black fabric, with a round opening on one side encircled by shining steel.

"A marvelous invention, the Kodak," said he, extricating a square brown envelope from the wrapping. "It makes every man a Louis Daguerre, without the expense of maintaining a processing laboratory. One has but to snap away until the rolled film is exposed, then send the camera to the company headquarters in America, where it is opened, the film is developed, and camera and pictures are returned by the next post. With the aid of Mr. Fulton's equally marvellous steamship, a British subject can expect to view the results within a month."

As he spoke, Holmes drew a sheaf of glossy photographic paper from the envelope, and there on that scrofulous street in modern London, we three gazed upon page after page of writing which few men had laid eyes on since before the fall of Rome.

Sir Richard Burton, seated at one of the desks in his study in a worn fez and an equally venerable dressing-gown of heavy Chinese silk, shuffled through the photographs like a seer reading the Tarot. His predatory eyes were bright.

"The bounder's a passing good photographer, thank the Lord for that," said he. "Shot ten pages at a time, and with some enlargement and the help of a good glass, I should be able to decipher them all. How in thunder did you work it out?"

"His brief infatuation with the Kodak stood out against the indolent portrait you painted," Holmes said. "When you referred to his trips to the corner post office, the thing was fairly settled for me. What interest can a disinherited man, recently dismissed and without prospects, have in the post? I withheld my suspicions until I could examine the vicinity where the theft took place. The scrap of parchment near the hearth, and the missing camera, eliminated any other theory which might have proposed itself."

"You have rescued history."

"Tish-tosh. I have merely saved you the price of Patterson's extortion. He would almost certainly have approached you with the pictures, as you surmised. In any case, the credit is as much Watson's as mine. You'd have done well to have so nimble a companion in Africa."

"If I'd had you both, I'd have tracked the blasted Nile to its cradle," he grumbled. "You let Patterson go?"

"I thought it best the record of Tutankhamen's tomb remain with you than in the evidence room at Scotland Yard. I did him no service. Eventually he will commit a crime for which no one can or will absolve him."

Burton studied each photograph in turn a second time. At last he set them down and rose, offering Holmes his hand. "I wish I'd known you in '60."

"You would not have found me diverting company, Sir Richard. I was six years old."

The case which I have indulged myself so far as to call "The Adventure of the Arabian Knight" has shed more light upon the singular methods of Sherlock Holmes than upon the undefiled resting-place of an Egyptian Pharaoh. Twenty-six months after the events herinfore described, Sir Richard Burton died, a victim of a combination of ailments he'd contracted during his many explorations into places which before him were unknown to white society. His loss was regretted in some quarters, celebrated in others. History, in which he placed so much store, will determine whether he was a serious scholar or a reckless adventurer bent only on sensation.

In order to protect her late husband's reputation from malicious gossip connected to some manuscripts she found morally objectionable, Lady Isabel Burton burned most of his voluminous papers. Among them, it must be concluded, since nothing has since been heard of them, were the photographs James Patterson took of the Egyptian document and any notes Burton may have made subsequent to their recovery. In view of this calamity, it seems likely that King Tut's tomb will remain forever buried beneath the sand of many centuries.

John H. Watson

10 May 1904

THE ADVENTURE OF THE THREE GHOSTS

"Compliments of the season, Watson. I note Lady Featherstone retains her childhood infatuation with you. She thinks you twelve feet tall and two yards wide at the shoulders."

Scarcely had I entered the ground floor at 221B Baker Street and surrendered my outerwear to the redoubtable Mrs. Hudson when I was thus greeted by Sherlock Holmes, who stood upon the landing outside the flat we'd shared for so long. He wore his prized old mouse-colored dressing-gown, and his eyes were brighter than usual.

"Good Lord, Holmes," said I, climbing the stairs. "How could you know I saw Constance Featherstone this morning? Her invitation to breakfast was the first contact I have had with her since the wedding."

"You forget, dear fellow, that I know your wardrobe as well as your wife does. I can hardly be expected not to notice a new muffler, particularly when it bears the Dornoch tartan. You told me once in a loquacious humour of your early romance with Constance Dornoch. Who but she would present you with such a token in honour of the holiday? And who but a sentimental lady who still thought you taller and broader than the common breed of man would knot one so long and bulky that it wound five times round your not inconsiderable neck and stood out like the oaken collar of a Mongolian slave?"

I simply shook my head, for to remark upon my friend's preternatural powers of observation and deduction would be merely to repeat myself for the thousandth time. Ensconced presently in my old armchair in the dear old cluttered sitting-room I knew so well, I accepted a glass of whisky to draw the December chill from my bones and enquired what he was up to at present.

"Your timing is opportune," said he, folding his long limbs into the basket chair, where with his hands resting upon his knees he bore no small resemblance to an East Indian shaman. "In ten minutes I shall hail a hansom to carry me to an address on Threadneedle Street, where I fully expect my fare to be paid by the Earl of Chislehurst."

I nodded, not greatly impressed, although Lord Chislehurst was a respected Member of Parliament and a frequent weekend guest at Balmoral, and whispered about as the Queen's favoured candidate for Minister of Finance. In the hierarchy of Holmes's clients, which had included a pontiff, a Prime Minister of England, and a foreign king, a noble banker placed fairly low. "A problem involving money?" I asked.

"No, a haunting. Are you interested?"

I responded that I most certainly was; and ten minutes later, my friend having exchanged his dressing-gown for an ulster, warm woollen muffler, and his favourite earflapped travelling cap, we were in a hansom rolling and sliding over the icy pavement through a gentle fall of snow. Vendors were hawking roast chestnuts, and over everything, the grim grey buildings and the holiday shoppers hurrying to and fro, bearing armloads of brightly wrapped packages, there had settled a festive atmosphere which transformed our dreary old London into a magical kingdom. In two days it would be gone, along with Christmas itself, but for the moment it lightened the heart and gilded it with hope.

"The earl is not a fanciful man," explained Holmes, holding on to the side of the conveyance. "A decade ago he acquired a money-lending institution teetering on the precipice of ruin and within a few short years brought it to the point where it is now universally thought of as one of the ten or twelve most reliable banking firms in England. Such men do not take lightly to ghosts."

I could divine no more detail than this, as very soon we pulled up before a gloomy old pile which I suspected had shown no great ceremony in its construction under George III, and to which the lapse of nearly a century and a half had brought little in the way of dignity or character. It seemed a most unlikely shelter for the institution Holmes had described.

Lord Chislehurst, to whom we were shown by a distracted young clerk, ameliorated to a great extent this disappointing impression. Well along in his fifties, he had yet a youthful abundance of fair hair, with but a trace of grey in the side whiskers, and the gracefully swelling abdomen that instilled confidence in those who would trust their fortunes to the care of one so well fed, contained in a grey waistcoat and black frock coat. His broad face was flushed and his manner cordial as he exhorted us to make ourselves comfortable in a pair of deep leather chairs facing his great desk. I noticed as he made his way round to his own seat that he walked with a pronounced limp.

"I am doubly honoured, Dr. Watson, to welcome you to my place of business," said he, leaning back and threading his fingers together across his middle. "I have read your published accounts of Mr. Holmes's cases with a great deal of interest. As a writer, you may be intrigued to learn that my father toiled for many years as a clerk in the counting-house you came through just now."

"You have done well for yourself," I said truthfully.

"So my father might say. Despite the hardship, he was a jovial man, and would laugh long and loud to see his youngest child making free with the cigars in this office." He helped himself to one from a cherrywood box upon the desk and proffered the rest, but we declined.

"Hardship?" prompted Holmes.

"The former owner was a fierce old ogre in his time, and pinched the halfpenny till it shrieked. Changed quite a bit in his last years, though, I'll be bound; saw the light, I suspect, as Judgement neared. His generosity to his employees after that made it possible for Father to arrange an operation that saved my life. I was a sickly child—a cripple, in fact. Unfortunately, the old banker overdid himself in the largesse department, and wound up sacrificing those same sound business principles that made him wealthy. His fortunes declined even as mine ascended. He died in debt, and I acquired the firm the very week I entered the Peerage."

Holmes lit a cigarette. "An inspiring story, Your Lordship. Your letter—"

"The tea is not always sweet," he interrupted. "I had hoped to move the offices to more suitable quarters down the street next spring, but this South African mess has got all our foreign securities tied up. Against my better judgement, I have been forced to cancel this year's employee gratuities."

"Your letter mentioned a ghost."

"Three ghosts, Mr. Holmes. As if one were not sufficient." Our host's genial smile had vanished. "I have been visited by them the past two nights, and I must say it's getting to be a dashed nuisance."

"What happened the first night?"

"I was not greatly alarumed by it, thinking the business a bad dream caused by exhaustion and overindulgence. That day had been long and frustrating, beginning with more bad news from Africa in the *Times*, and complicated by a discrepancy in the accounts totalling forty-two pounds, which required that the transactions of the entire week be gone over with a weather eye by everyone on the staff. When the error was finally discovered and the correction made, the hour was well past seven. As is my wont, I stopped at the tavern round the corner on my way home, where I confess I had rather more than my customary tot of sherry. My wife, recognising my condition at the door, put me to bed straightaway.

"I slept as one dead until the stroke of one, at which time I awoke, or thought I awoke, with the realisation that I was not alone in my chamber."

"One moment," interrupted Holmes. "You do not share sleeping quarters with your wife?"

"Not since the early months of our marriage. I often sleep fitfully, with much tossing and muttering, and my wife is a light sleeper. I prefer not to disturb her. Is it significant?"

"Perhaps not. Please proceed."

"'Who is there?' I asked groggily; for I was aware of a shimmering paleness in a corner of the room that was usually dark, as of a shaft of moonlight reflecting off a human face.

"'The Ghost of Christmas Past,' came the reply. The voice was most solemn but youthful, and very much of this earth.

"'Whose past?' I demanded. 'Who let you in?'"

"'Your past,' said the shade; and then some rot about coming along with him."

Holmes, settled deep in his chair with his lower limbs stretched in front of him and his eyes closed, said nothing, listening. His cigarette smoked between his fingers. As for myself, I felt my brow wrinkling. The narrative had begun to sound familiar.

"The rest is quite personal," the earl continued. "Vivid memories of my childhood, Christmas dinner with my mother and father and my brother Peter and my sister Martha, and Father going on about a goose, and what-have-you. Obviously I was dreaming, but I had the distinct impression of having travelled a great distance, and that I was peeping at all this as through a window, with the Ghost of Christmas Past standing at my elbow. It was all very strange, but nice, and sad as well. My parents are dead, my sister married and gone to America, and my brother and I have not spoken in years. We quarrelled over our meagre inheritance. I suppose it is not unusual to feel wistful over the happier days of youth. Still, it was an odd coincidence."

Holmes opened his eyes. "How was it a coincidence?"

"I had spent much of that trying day shut up with Richard, my chief clerk, going over the accounts. When at length the discrepancy I mentioned was identified and corrected, it seemed natural to invite him to join me in a glass of sherry at the tavern. He accepted, and we whiled away a convivial evening reminiscing about Christmasses old and new. So it seems odd that I should dream about the very same thing that night."

"Not at all, Your Lordship," I put in. "Man is a suggestible creature. It would be far more unusual to dream about something that was not in one's mind recently."

"I think there is something in what you say, Doctor. Certainly it would help to explain the second part of my dream." The Earl lit a fresh cigar, apparently forgetting the one he had left smouldering only half-smoked in the tray on his desk. "It seems I returned to my bed, for again the clock struck one and I found myself as I had previously, staring at a phosphorescence in the corner and asking what was there.

"'The Ghost of Christmas Present,' responded a most remarkable voice, jolly and full of timbre, as of a man in the fullness of his middle years. Just this, and again the summons to come along.

"Now we were standing outside the window of a tiny flat in the City, witnessing what appeared to be a serious row between a young husband and his wife over money; something about not having sufficient funds to settle their bills, let alone celebrate the holiday. At the tavern, Richard had told me of a number of financial setbacks they had suffered because of unforeseen emergencies, but I had not perceived how serious the situation was until that moment. It appeared to threaten their union."

"Had you met his wife?" Holmes asked.

"I have not had that pleasure. However, he keeps a photographic portrait of her at his desk. She is most comely."

"Women generally are, in photographs. What happened when the clock again struck one?"

Lord Chislehurst permitted himself an arid smile. "I should have been disappointed had you not seen the pattern. This phantom, who indicated through gestures that he was the Ghost of Christmas Yet to Come, was the most unsettling of all, and the picture he showed me of some future Yuletide was bleak and hideous. I saw Richard's home broken, his wife, stigmatised by divorce, forced to make her living from the streets, even as Richard pursued a bitter and lonely existence as an unloved and aging bachelor. Worse, I saw my own neglected grave. Evidently I had gone to it without obsequy, my harsh and penurious business practices having ruined lives and left none to mourn my passing." He shuddered.

Holmes finished his cigarette. "In your waking moments, My Lord, are you given to dwelling morbidly upon the subject of your future demise?"

"Never. I regard it as an inevitability, which to brood over is to squander what little life we have. This was what I told Lady Chislehurst when she brought up the subject of my last will and testament."

"Indeed?" Holmes lifted his brows. "Did this discussion take place before or after your dream?"

"Before. That very night, in fact. When I was late coming home from the tavern, she entertained various concerns over what might have befallen me, as wives will. When I arrived at last, she expressed relief, then scolded me as I was preparing to retire that I should be more careful, as the streets are not safe at night for a man not in full possession of his wits, and that if I insisted upon placing myself in jeopardy I should make arrangements for the division of my estate before some footpad separates me from my watch and my life."

"A practical woman."

"Very much so. It is the quality which drew my attention to her in the first place. I met her when she came to work for me as a typist. Her suggestions for the improvement of the firm were inspired, and as she was of good family I soon realised that she was the woman to bring order to my existence away from the office. We were married within a year. From time to time, when the firm is shorthanded due to illness or personal emergency among the staff, she still comes in to help out."

"I assume she works well with Richard."

"They make an ideal team. Often I have seen them in conference, with many nods and expressions of agreement. But what has this to do with my ghosts?"

"Probably nothing. Perhaps everything. Let us return to this will. Were you persuaded to make it out?"

"My solicitor was in this morning. I signed the documents and Richard witnessed my signature. My wife is chief beneficiary, and Richard is executor; he is a reliable man, and the fee will come in handy should his financial difficulties continue."

"I commend Your Lordship upon his generosity. You had the dream again last night?"

"Yes, and I'm not certain it was a dream. I was cold sober, having gone straight home from the office without stopping at the tavern, and retired at a decent hour. A cup of tea with Lady Chislehurst before bed was my only indulgence. I shall not repeat myself, for the visitations were the same, including the redundant striking of the hour of one upon the clock, the shades of Christmasses Past, Present, and Yet to Come, and the visions which accompanied them. This time, however, it was all much more vivid. I awoke this morning with the conviction that it had all been true. And there was something else, Mr. Holmes: the condition of my bedroom slippers."

"Your bedroom slippers?"

"Yes." He leaned forwards, placing his palms upon his desk. "They were soaked through, Mr. Holmes, exactly as if I had been walking in snow the whole night."

This intelligence had a profound effect upon my friend. Face thrust forwards now, his eyes keen and his nostrils flaring, he said, "I must prevail upon Your Lordship to invite Dr. Watson and myself to be your guests tonight."

The earl frowned—less perturbed, I thought, by the inconvenience of entertaining two unexpected houseguests as by the impropriety of Holmes having made the suggestion himself. "You deem this necessary?"

"I consider it of the utmost importance."

"Very well. I shall send a messenger to inform my wife."

"That is precisely what I must ask you not to do. No one must know that we are in residence."

"May I ask why?"

"Everything depends upon the outward appearance that your nightly routine remains unchanged. I assure you I am not being melodramatic when I say your life is in danger."

"But of what, Mr. Holmes? By whom?"

Holmes stood, ignoring this reasonable question. "I shall need time to lay my trap. Will it be possible to ensure that Lady Chislehurst and your servants are all away from home this evening between the hours of eight and nine?"

"That should not be difficult. Our cook will have left by then, and our maid is away visiting relatives for the holiday. I shall suggest my wife call upon her friend Mrs. Wesley down the street. She was widowed last spring and faces a lonely Christmas."

"Excellent. Pray inform her that you are exhausted and will probably have retired by the time she returns. Dr. Watson and I shall be watching from cover. Expect us immediately after she has gone. It is extremely important that you share none of these details with anyone, especially your clerk."

The earl was plainly troubled, but agreed without further questions, and provided us with directions to his London lodgings, whereupon we moved towards the door. Upon the threshold I turned and said, "I should like to ask Your Lordship a question, a personal one."

"I have no secrets, Doctor."

"Is your family name by any chance Cratchit?"

He appeared surprised. "Why, yes, it is. I was born Timothy Cratchit. Did you read that in Brook's?"

"No, Your Lordship; in Dickens."

Lord Chislehurst scowled. "That miserable yarn-spinner! I personally have not read his invasive little story, yet I cannot escape from it. Until I entered the nobility I could go nowhere without some new acquaintance hailing me as Tiny Tim, despite having achieved my full growth, and thinking himself quite the clever fellow. I'd have the meddler in court were he still living."

After we had been shown out of the counting-room by Richard, who seemed a personable sort, well-groomed and -dressed within the limitations of a clerk's salary, Holmes asked me the meaning of the last exchange.

I was stupefied. "Surely you are familiar with Charles Dickens's 'A Christmas Carol'! Every English schoolboy has had the story force-fed to him each December since it made its appearance."

"I was an uncommon schoolboy, and I haven't the faintest notion as to what you are referring."

Briefly, in the hansom on the way back to Baker Street, I summarised that most English of Christmas tales and its unforgettable cast of characters: Ebenezer Scrooge, the miserly, holiday-loathing banker; Bob Cratchit, his long-suffering clerk; Cratchit's loveable, crippled younger son, Tiny Tim; and the three ghosts who visited Scrooge and brought about his conversion to the season of love and forgiveness. Holmes listened with keen interest.

"I recall telling you once that it is a mistake to imagine that one's brain-attic has elastic walls, and that the time will come when for every new shipment of information one accepts, another must be sacrificed," he said when I had finished. "However, I rather think I have an uncluttered corner still, and it seems to me that literature would not be an unwise thing to deposit there. What one man can invent, another can subvert.

If you and I are not careful tonight, Watson, your Mr. Dickens may well be an unwitting accomplice before the fact of murder."

"Whom do you suspect, and what is the motive?"

"Chiefly, I suspect Lady Chislehurst and Richard, the clerk. Whether their alliance is amorous or strictly mercenary has yet to be determined, but I am convinced they are in it together, and that Lord Chislehurst's estate is their object."

"But why the clerk? The wife is the sole beneficiary."

"It was he who planted the suggestion in the earl's mind which led to his Christmas Present vision of strife in Richard's household. Our client was not aware of his subordinate's dire financial situation before their most timely conversation. There is nothing so effective as a little haunting, abetted by an application of strong spirits and combined with a wife's reminder of one's fiscal responsibilities to his family, for bringing a man to a contemplation of his mortality, and to the arrangement for the disposition of his worldly goods."

"Are you suggesting he was mesmerised?"

"I suspect something even more ambitious and diabolical. You may count upon it, Watson, there is skullduggery afoot. I am reminded most acutely of that business at the Baskerville estate during the early years of our association. If there is a ghost involved here at all, it is that blackguard Stapleton's."

At this point Holmes fell into a dark reverie, from which I knew from long experience he would not be drawn until the hour of our appointment with our endangered client. As we clip-clopped homeward through those streets laden with snow, the seasonal spirit was significantly absent inside that cab.

Big Ben had just struck eight, and the resonance of its final chime was still in the air when a well-built woman in her middle years bustled out the doorway of an imposing pile not far from Threadneedle Street and started down the pavement wrapped in a heavy cloak. This, I assumed, was Lady Chislehurst; and she had not been out of sight thirty seconds when Holmes and I emerged from the shallow doorway across the street where we had stationed ourselves five minutes previously.

Holmes did not ring the bell right away, but paced the length of the front of the building, swinging his cane in the metronomic manner he often used to measure distance. Presently he climbed the front steps with me at his heels.

The bell was answered almost immediately by our client, whose attire of nightcap and dressing-gown assured us he had followed Holmes's advice and convinced his wife that he was retiring. Once we were admitted to the rather dark and gloomy foyer, the detective repeated the procedure he had conducted outside, pacing the room deliberately from the left wall to the right.

"An interesting building," he said when he was standing before the earl once again. "James the First, is it not?"

"James the Second, or so I was told when I acquired it from the Scrooge estate. It was a depressing old place, neglected and in disrepair. Lady Chislehurst has done much to improve it, although much remains to be done. The very first thing she did was to see to it that the hideous old door-knocker was removed. The lion's head frightened our nieces and nephews when they came to visit."

"It is admirable of you both to take the trouble to preserve the place. The loss of such an unusually substantial example of architecture would be a great tragedy. There is a difference of six feet in the width of the building between the outside and the inside. One seldom encounters walls three feet thick so far past the medieval period."

"Indeed. I never noticed."

"I am always intrigued by how little attention we pay to familiar things, which are to us the most important. May we inspect your chamber?"

We were led up a narrow flight of stairs to a large room on the first floor, equipped with a huge old four-poster bed and a stone fireplace nearly large enough to walk into upright, with a bearskin stretched before it on the hearth. Above the mantel hung a huge old painting in a gilt frame of a medieval noblewoman languishing on the floor of a dungeon, with light streaming down upon her from a barred window high on the wall.

"An outside room," observed Holmes. "Do you not find it draughty?"

"No; the window was bricked in years ago."

"Convenient."

"How so, Mr. Holmes?"

"Darkness, of course. There is nothing less conducive to sleep than an unwanted shaft of light. Is that the corner in which you saw the apparitions? Yes, that is where they would be most visible to someone sitting up in bed. Where is Lady Chislehurst's chamber in relation to yours?"

"Just down the hall. Do you wish to see it?"

"That won't be necessary." He swung upon our host, eyes bright as twin beacons. "Dr. Watson dabbles a bit in Jamesian architecture. Would Your Lordship object to conducting him upon a tour while I complete my inspection? I thought not. Thank you for your hospitality."

"Curious fellow, your Mr. Holmes," said the earl when we were in the gaslit hallway outside the room where Holmes could be heard rummaging about. "Is he always this unusual?"

"Usually."

"Do you know anything at all about Jamesian architecture?"

"Only that it is uncommon to find walls so thick, and I didn't know that until a few minutes ago."

He produced two cigars from the pocket of his dressing-gown and gave me one. "Curious fellow."

"He is the best detective in England."

We had smoked a third of our cigars when the door opened. Holmes appeared sanguine, as if he had spent the time stretched out upon the bed. "There you are, Watson. Does Your Lordship have a spare bedroom?"

"I have several. Would you and the doctor like to share one, or would you prefer separate quarters?"

"With your permission, we shall share yours. I am suggesting that you sleep in the spare room."

"Whatever for?"

Holmes smiled and placed a finger to his lips.

"As Dr. Watson has no doubt told you, my methods are my own and I seldom confide them. Pray do as I ask, and do not venture out under any circumstances. By morning I hope to have laid your ghosts to rest."

"See here, Holmes," said I when we were alone in the room. "I have known you far too long to accept this nonsense about architecture as an adequate explanation for keeping secrets from me. What were you about while I was out on that fool's errand?"

My friend had removed his boots and stripped to his shirtsleeves and was making himself comfortable upon the big four-poster. "Forgive me, dear fellow. You know full well my weakness for theatrics. In any case your own mind is too active for you to continue to assist me in these little problems if I fail to occupy it. I have come to depend upon my amusements. What was lightning before Franklin arrived with his kite and key? Merely a pretty display."

My disgruntlement was only partly relieved by this pedantic apology. "What do we do now?"

"Nothing."

"Nothing?!"

"Turn down the lamp, will you? There's a good fellow." Whereupon, in the dim orange glow of the lowered wick of the lamp upon the bed-side table, he closed his eyes. Within moments his even breathing told me he was asleep.

I did not join him in the arms of Morpheus. Although nothing had been said, I knew from past experience that one of us must remain vigilant, and so I stayed awake in the room's one chair, feeling the reassuring solidity of my faithful service revolver in my pocket.

At length I heard the front door open and shut, and divined that Lady Chislehurst had returned from her visit. Presently, light footsteps climbed the stairs, paused briefly outside the room as if waiting for some sign of movement from within, whilst I held my breath; then they continued down the hall, where the snick and then the thump of a door opening and closing told me that our client's wife had returned to her room. Then silence.

The night wore on. The room was chill without a fire, for which I was grateful, as it kept me alert. The shadows thrown by the nearly nonexistent light were monstrous, and in my imagination I peopled them with all sorts of mortal terrors.

I must have dozed, despite the cold, for I was suddenly aware of a pale light in a corner of the room where before there had been only darkness, and I had the impression it had been there for some little time. I started, and reached instantly for my revolver. However, a sudden sharp sibilant from the direction of the bed halted me. Holmes was sitting up, his attention centred on the light in the corner. His profile was predatory in its silver reflection.

As we watched, the light changed, assuming vaguely human shape. Now we were looking at a tall, gaunt figure seemingly wrapped in a cloak as black as the shadows that surrounded it. Its face was invisible in the depths of the cowl covering its head, but its skeletal wrist protruded from a loose sleeve, and as the image shimmered before us, its crooked, bony finger appeared to beckon.

My heart hammered in my breast. Clearly, this was the most frightening phantasm of the three that had been described to us; the Ghost of Christmas Yet to Come, with its cold, silent promise of a lonely grave for he who encountered it.

"Quick, Watson! The light!"

I hesitated but briefly, then reached over and turned up the lamp. Immediately the ghost vanished. I leapt to my feet, starting in that direction. Holmes, however, moved to the wall adjacent, which contained the huge fireplace. The grate was supported by an enormous pair of andirons of medieval manufacture, one of which he seized by its lion's-head ornament and pulled towards himself. There was a pause, followed by a grating sound, as of a rusted gate opening upon hinges disused for decades. Then the entire back of the fireplace, which I had assumed to be constructed of solid stone, slid sideways, exposing a black hollow beyond.

"A passageway!" said I.

"I surmised as much from the beginning. You will remember I remarked upon the discrepancy between the inside and outside measurements of the building. Hand me the lamp, and keep your revolver handy. Remove your boots. We don't want them to know we're coming."

I did as directed. Holding the light aloft, Holmes stepped over the grate and into the blackness, with me close upon his heels.

The passage was narrow, dank, and musky-smelling. Once inside, Holmes exclaimed softly and lifted the lamp higher. A great metal contraption equipped with a glass lens stood upon a ledge at shoulder height. I smelled molten wax.

"It looks like a lantern," I whispered.

"A *magic* lantern; or so it is fancifully known." Standing upon tiptoe, Holmes reached up with his free hand, groped at the contraption, and slid a pane of glass from a slot behind the lens. He examined it briefly, then handed it to me. When I held it up against the light of the lamp, I recognized the image of our old friend the Ghost of Christmas Yet to Come etched upon the glass.

"The image is projected through the lens when the candle is lit," Holmes explained. "When I examined the room earlier, I found a small hole in the painting above the mantel, just where the light streams through the window to fall upon the lady in the dungeon. That is where our ghost gained access to the room. When I found the mechanism that opens the fireplace, I knew my suspicions were correct. I daresay if we look, we shall find similar panes bearing the likenesses of the Ghosts of Christmas Past and Present precisely as they were described to us."

"But Past and Present spoke to the earl!"

"It might surprise you to learn what a ghastly effect the echoes in a narrow passage such as this will lend to an ordinary human voice. But come!"

I was forced to hasten lest he outrun the light from the lamp. When I caught up with him several yards down that gloomy path, he was peering at a small bottle perched in a niche in the wall. Presently he removed it and held it out, asking me what I made of it.

"*Radix pedis diaboli*," I read from the label. The old familiar name clamped my heart in an icy fist.

"I see that you have not forgotten the grim affair of the Tregennis murders. No doubt you remember also the rather melodramatic title under which you published your account of them."

I shuddered. "'The Adventure of the Devil's Foot'! But the Devil's-foot root is a deadly poison!"

"It is also a hallucinogen in small doses. Small enough, let's say, to escape notice once it has been introduced into one's sherry."

"Richard," I whispered. "Lord Chislehurst told us his clerk accompanied him to his tavern for a glass the night the ghosts first visited."

"I suspected him the moment the earl told us how Richard had taken him into his confidence about his financial situation. That, and the picture of Richard's wife in the counting-room, planted a suggestion in our client's mind. Under the influence of the root tincture, it came back to him in his dreams, convincing him that Christmas Present was allowing him a peep into his employee's private life."

"But how do you explain the glimpse that Christmas Past provided into his own childhood?"

"Christmas is a time of remembering, Watson. No doubt the earl was reminded of his own impoverished origins, which sprang forth as a vision at the mere mention of the word *past*. Post-mesmeric suggestion is a fascinating scientific phenomenon. I should like to know how Richard came by his expertise, or if the talent was inbred. It would make an interesting subject for a monograph."

"One moment, Holmes! His Lordship was haunted the same way last night, yet he said he came straight home from work. His clerk had not the opportunity to administer the drug again."

"But Her Ladyship did. He said himself he had a cup of tea with her before retiring."

"You're certain they're in it together? Richard and Lady Chislehurst?"

His expression was grave.

"It was she who insisted her husband prepare his will without delay. She is the beneficiary, but Richard is the Svengali in our little melodrama. 'What evil one may do compounds when they are two.' They already have our unfortunate client walking the streets in his sleep—mark you his sopping slippers! Who is there to say, when he is found some night murdered in an alley, that he was not set upon by some anonymous ruffian while in the somnambulant state?"

"Good Lord! And in the season of love and mercy!"

Holmes hissed for silence. Motioning for me to follow, he crept along the inside wall, and I realised belatedly that he was measuring the distance. Presently he stepped away as far as the outside wall would permit, scrutinising the other from ceiling to floor. He seized a stony protuberance and, with a significant nod towards the revolver in my hand, pushed with all his might. Again there was a grating noise, and then a section of wall eight feet high and four feet wide swung outwards upon a hidden pivot. Light flooded the passage. Together we stepped through.

We were in a chamber slightly smaller than Lord Chislehurst's, with a cosy fireplace, a bed piled high with pillows and canopied in chintz and ivory lace, a dressing-table, and a huge oak cabinet quite as old as the house, before which stood a tall, handsome woman ten years our client's junior, fully dressed and coiffed in a manner both expensive and tasteful. She appeared composed, but upon her cheeks was a high colour.

"Lady Chislehurst, if I may be so bold?" Holmes enquired.

"That is my name, sir. Who are you, and what is the meaning of this invasion?"

"My name is Sherlock Holmes. This is Dr. Watson, and unless I am very much mistaken, the gentleman hiding in the cabinet is named Richard."

Her hand went to her throat. She took an involuntary step closer to the cabinet. "Sir! You are impertinent."

"Just so; and yet so far it has not proven a failing in my work. Will you open the door, or has the gentleman the moral fibre to present himself and spare you that indignity?"

At that moment, the door to the cabinet opened and a slender young man stepped out. I recognised Lord Chislehurst's clerk, dressed in black from collar to heels. I raised my revolver.

"That won't be necessary, Doctor. I am unarmed." He spread his dark coattails, revealing the truth of his assertion. I returned my weapon to my pocket, but kept my hand upon it warily.

"I fled from the passage when the fireplace opened," Richard explained. "Not knowing who might be in the hall, and fearful of compromising Lady Chislehurst, I took refuge in the cabinet. I thought perhaps it was the earl, and that we had been found out."

"So you have. You admit that you were conspiring to murder Lord Chislehurst?" Holmes's tone was sepulchral.

The woman gasped and swayed. Richard put out his arm to steady her. His face was white. "Good heavens, no! However did you form that conclusion?"

"Come, come, young man. There is the business of the will, the paraphernalia in the passage between the walls, and your own admission just now that you feared you had been 'found out.' I suggest you hold your defense in reserve for the Assizes."

"Thank you, Richard. I am quite well now." The lady relinquished her grip upon the young man's arm. Her expression was resolute. "You are quite mistaken, Mr. Holmes, as to our motives and intentions. I have been after Timothy for years to arrange his estate. I saw no reason that the fortune he has worked so hard to build should be dissipated in the courts. To whom he decided to leave it was his own affair, but I thought it would be appropriate if he named Richard as executor.

"I have known Richard for two years. I don't think my husband realises how valuable he has been to the firm, nor how much of himself he has sacrificed to its operation. This I know from what I have seen. Richard does not advertise his worth."

"Please, Your Ladyship," protested the clerk.

She smiled at him sadly, dismissing his plea. "When you work closely with someone, as I have with Richard when the firm was shorthanded, you learn things his employer doesn't know. Richard's financial situation is heinous. Aside from his responsibilities as a husband, he has pledged to repay the many debts left by his late father, and his mother is seriously ill.

"Richard is the first member of his family to pursue a career in business," she continued. "His father was a mesmerist upon the stage, and his mother was a magician's assistant. When I learned that he had inherited some of their skills, a plan began to materialise."

The clerk interrupted. "The plan was mine. Lady Chislehurst went along purely out of the goodness of her heart."

"You needn't claim responsibility," said she. "I'm proud of the idea. My husband is a good man, Mr. Holmes, but his order of values is not always sound. When the firm suffered, he should have chosen an area to practise economy that would not affect his employees. When he told me there would be no Christmas gratuities this year, I knew from experience I could not change his mind through talk. I decided instead to work upon his conscience. I suppose you know the rest."

Holmes appeared unmoved.

"Your plan was dangerous, Madame. Any number of tragedies might have befallen your husband as he wandered in his sleep."

"That was unexpected, and alarumed me greatly." Her expression was remorseful. "It did not happen the first time. I obtained the Devil's-foot herb from Richard, but I misheard his instructions and misjudged the amount I put in Timothy's tea. Afterwards, Richard and I decided not to use the drug again. If the mere image of the Ghost of Christmas Yet to Come did not bring about the desired conversion, that was that."

"I am shamed." This was a new voice.

"Timothy!" Lady Chislehurst turned to face her husband, who was standing upon the threshold to the hallway. None of us had seen him open the door, with the possible exception of Holmes, whose red-Indian countenance betrayed no reaction.

"I am not shamed for you," he added hastily, "but for myself. Were I not so caught up in commerce, I would have seen what effect my measures to preserve the firm was having upon the people I depend upon."

His wife stepped towards him just as he strode forwards. He took her in his arms. "I'm sorry, Beth. Can you ever forgive me?"

"There is one way," said she.

"Of course." He looked at his clerk. "Richard, I want you in early tomorrow."

The young man was dismayed. "Tomorrow is Christmas Day!"

"All the more reason to start early, so we can count out the holiday gratuities, beginning with yours. If we work hard we should be able to deliver them all by midday. Then you and your wife will join us here for Christmas dinner. Mrs. MacTeague has a fair way with a goose and plum pudding, and the claret the late Mr. Scrooge put down in '39 should be at its peak."

"Bless you, sir!"

"Bless *you*, Beth!"

"God bless us everyone!" I exclaimed.

Four curious faces turned my way.

"Surely you are more familiar with those words than most," I told the earl and his wife. "Lady Chislehurst especially. She must have studied 'A Christmas Carol' closely whilst engineering her little conspiracy."

"I haven't read it in years. My husband doesn't approve of the story. I thought about it, naturally, but my real inspiration came when I discovered the secret passage and the equipment inside."

Holmes said, "Do you mean to say the apparatus was there already?"

"The magic lantern is an old model," explained Richard: "an ancestor, as it were, of the ones employed by the magicians with whom my mother performed. I replaced the bottle of hallucinative with one my father used in his act. The original would have been useless. It had probably been there forty years."

"That is precisely when Scrooge lived here," reflected the earl.

"Well, Watson, what do you make of our little Yuletide adventure?"

The next morning was Christmas. After I had breakfasted and exchanged greetings and gifts with my wife, I paid a call upon Holmes in the old sitting-room, where I found him enjoying his morning pipe.

"I should say Bob Cratchit was fortunate there was no Sherlock Holmes in his day," said I.

"Crafty fellows, these clerks. However, they are no match for a Lady Chislehurst. I perceive that package you are carrying is intended for me, by the way. The shops are closed, Mrs. Hudson is away visiting, and you know no one else in this neighbourhood."

I handed him the bundle, wrapped in brown paper and tied with a cord.

"It is useless to try to surprise you, Holmes. It is a first-edition copy of *The Martyrdom of Man*, which you once recommended to me. I came across it in a secondhand shop in Soho."

His expression was pleased, but I detected a cloud behind it. "Splendid, but I'd rather hoped it would be 'A Christmas Carol.' This adventure has demonstrated to me that I've fallen behind in my reading."

It was with no small satisfaction that I reached into my coat pocket and handed him the story, bound in green calfskin with the title wreathed in gold.

He appeared nonplussed, a singular event.

"I am afraid, old fellow, that I have no gift to offer in return. The season has been busy, and as you know I allow little time for sentiment. It is disastrous to my work."

It may have been my interpretation only, but he sounded apologetic. I smiled.

"My dear Holmes. What greater gift could I receive than the one you have given me these many years?"

He returned the smile. "Happy Christmas, Watson."

"Happy Christmas, Holmes."

THE RIDDLE OF
THE GOLDEN
MONKEYS

t is a common misapprehension of old age that the widower is of necessity a lonely man even in the press of a crowd. In the third year of the reign of George V, I had been in bereavement for the better part of a decade, and the tragic inroads that had been made upon the British male population during the wars in South Africa and China were such that for a solitary gentleman in relatively good fettle to show himself in society was to trumpet his availability to any number of unattached women of a certain age.

This situation was exacerbated by the appearance, since the deaths of our gracious Victoria and that good-hearted man Edward VII, of a breed of bold, independent female who would step up and declare her intentions before a teeming ballroom with no more blushes than a tiger stalking a hare. The struggle for women's suffrage and unstable conditions upon the Continent had stripped the gender of its traditional reserve.

By the summer of 1913, I had long since abandoned my shock at such behaviour, but I found it wearisome in the extreme. I had reached that time in life wherein a cigar, a snifter, and a good book quite fulfills one's dreams of bliss. However, to confess to it in the presence of one of these daring creatures must needs give offence, and ultimately lead to the undoing of one's good reputation, which in the end is all any of us ever has.

"I jumped—it seems," writes Conrad, in *Lord Jim*. The declaration is appropriate to the action I took that June, when in response to frequent invitations I bolted London for the South Downs and a holiday from eligibility in the company of my oldest and closest friend.

Those who are familiar with my published recollections may remember that Sherlock Holmes, after a lifetime of unique service to the mighty and humble, had retired to an existence of contemplation and bee farming in Sussex. The setting was isolated, and in lieu of neighbours the modest villa looked out upon the brittle Channel from a crest of severe chalk cliffs similar to those which are commonly associated with Dover. Keenly I anticipated this lonely (and unapologetically masculine) stretch of English coastline, and a reunion with the man with whom I had shared so many adventures. I disembarked from the train at Newhaven and engaged an automobile and driver to convey me along the twenty miles of seacoast ahead, light in heart.

Chugging along at a brisk fifteen miles per hour, I held on to my hat with one hand and the side of the Daimler with the other, remembering when a clattering ride in a horsedrawn hansom towards the scene of some impending tragedy represented the height of excitement for a man of any age.

We were slowing for the turn to the villa when I recognised the gaunt figure approaching at a trot with the sea at his back.

"Watson—good fellow, is that you? I am only just in receipt of your wire. We are but one more scientific improvement away from outdistancing even the genius of Mr. Morse."

Holmes wore a terry robe, untied, over a bathing costume. Plastered to his skeletal frame, the damp wool told me that retirement from public life had neither increased his appetite nor lessened his distaste for inaction. But for the grey in his hair and the thinning at the temples, he did not appear to have aged a day since the attempt was made on his life by the blackguard Count Sylvius ten years before. It was the very last investigation we shared, and my final visit to our dear old digs in Baker Street.

I, meanwhile, had grown absolutely stout, a victim of my comfortable armchair and the bill of fare at Simpson's. We remained as separate in our habits as at the beginning.

Years and weight notwithstanding, I alighted eagerly from the passenger's seat and seized his hand, which was iron-cold from his late immersion in the icy Channel. At close range I observed the creases at the corners of his razor-sharp eyes and the deep furrows from his Roman nose to his thin mouth, cut by time and concentration. He put me in mind of a Yankee cigar-store Indian left out in the weather.

"I hope I have not inconvenienced you," I said.

"Not nearly as much as you have inconvenienced your dog. I trust the kennel in Blackheath is a good one."

I was so astounded by the mention of Blackheath that for a moment I could not recall if I'd ever told him I owned a dog.

He laughed in that way which many thought mirthless. "Time has not changed you, nor age sharpened your wits. An old athlete such as yourself cannot resist a visit to the rugby field of his youth, hence that particular dark loam adhering to your left heel. Fullness of age and greatness of girth might prevent a casual excursion, but you would travel that far to board your dog; a bull, if I am any judge of the stray hairs upon your coat."

"It would appear an old detective such as yourself cannot resist the urge to detect, whatever his circumstances."

Again he laughed. "A very palpable hit." Before I could protest, he had paid my driver, relieved him of my Gladstone bag, and started up the path towards the house.

Presently we were in his parlour, he having bathed and put on the somewhat shabby tweeds of a country gentleman. The room was small but commodious, with a bay window overlooking the water and sufficient memorabilia strewn about to create the sensation that we were back at 221B. Here was the dilapidated Oriental slipper, from which he filled his pipe with a portion of his old shag; there the framed photograph of Irene Adler, and she in her grave these twenty years. I recognised the harpoon that had slain Black Peter Carey and the worn old revolver that had saved our lives upon more than one occasion, now demoted to a decoration on the wall above the hearth. A library of tattered beekeeping manuals filled the bookpress which had once contained his commonplace books. I asked him how his bees fared.

"Splendidly. Later I shall bring out the congenial mead I've developed from the honey. It may make amends for supper. My housekeeper is deceased, I have not yet replaced her, and my cooking skills are not on a level with my ratiocination. I say, old fellow, would you mind terribly if we have a third at table?"

"A client?" I smiled.

"A man in need of a favour, which in an unprotected moment I agreed to provide. You may find him entertaining company. He's in the way of being a colleague of yours."

"A physician? I've not practised in years. We shall not be able to converse in the same language."

"A writer; or have you retired from letters as well as medicine? Sax Rohmer is the rather outlandish name." Turning in his armchair, he rummaged among a jumble of books in a case which looked disturbingly like a child's coffin, and tossed a volume across to where I sat facing him upon a sagging divan.

I inspected the book. It was bound cheaply, with a paper slipcover bearing the sensational title *The Mystery of Dr. Fu-Manchu*. Holmes smoked his pipe in silence whilst I read the opening pages.

I closed the book and laid it in my lap. "I read this same story in serial form in a London magazine. I considered bringing suit against the author, but I couldn't decide whether to base it on grounds of invasion of privacy or base plagiarism."

"Indeed. I noticed the resemblance myself: a clipped-sounding adventurer with a pipe and a nervous manner and his storytelling companion, an energetic young physician. The late lamented Professor Moriarty might also have brought a case as regards this devil doctor. But the story itself is rather ingenious and, apart from borrowing your unfortunate practice of leaving out the most important bit of information until the last, his debt to your published memoirs seems negligible—altogether too fanciful to be taken as genuine. He sent me this inscribed advance copy along with his letter requesting my assistance."

I opened the book to the flyleaf and read: "To Sherlock Holmes, Esq., with admiration. Sax Rohmer." The *S* in "Sax" bore two vertical lines straight through it, in imitation of the American dollar sign.

Perhaps it was this boastful reference to the author's success upon both sides of the Atlantic that raised my ire. My own writings had required years of seasoning to attain critical and commercial acclaim.

"I never knew your head to be turned by flattery and a disingenuous gift," I said churlishly.

"Good Watson, it was the problem which turned my head. This old frame is far too brittle to support any further laurels. But here, I believe, is the gentleman himself. You nearly arrived upon the same train, and might have fought your duel on board."

Holmes opened the front door just as another automobile from town pulled away, greeted his visitor, and performed introductions. I was taken aback by the appearance of this straight, trim young fellow, whom I judged to be about thirty years of age; his aquiline features, keen gaze, and general air of self-possession reminded me uncannily of the eager young student of unidentified sciences who first shook my hand in the chemical laboratory of St. Bartholomew's Hospital, three decades and so many adventures ago. So close was the resemblance that I was startled into accepting his handshake. I had intended to be polite but cold and aloof.

"Dr. Watson," he said, "I'm quite as excited to make your acquaintance as I am that of Mr. Holmes. You cannot know what an inspiration you have been to me; though you would, in the unlikely event you were ever to read my work. I am a shameless imitator."

This confession—the very last thing I had expected from him—left me with neither speech nor ammunition. I had been prepared to accuse him of that same transgression, and for him to deny having committed it. In one brief, pretty declaration he had managed to turn a contemptible deed into an act of veneration.

I was not, however, disposed to respond to guile. I said, "You might first have sought the opinion of the imitated, to determine whether the honour would be welcome."

He nodded, as if he were considering the matter. "I might have, and I should. I can only state in my defence that I thought you existed on far too lofty a plane to be approached by one of my youth and inexperience. Pray accept my apology, and I shall post the circumstances of my debt to you upon the front page of the *Times*."

This sentiment, and the obvious sincerity with which it was delivered, unmasted me thoroughly. For all his seeming repose, young Rohmer was clearly flummoxed by the celebrated company in which he found himself. This was evident both by his attitude and by his dress; his Norfolk and whipcords, although quite correct to his surroundings, were new almost to the point of gaucherie. He had dressed to please, and his efforts to ingratiate himself touched that which remained of the youth inside me. I told him no public abasement was necessary, and in so doing informed him he was forgiven.

Moments later we were sharing the divan, enjoying the whiskies-and-soda which Holmes had prepared as carefully as his chemical experiments of old, and with considerably greater success than some. My friend—showing subtle signs of discomfort born of rheumatism—had assumed his Indian pose of listening, with legs folded and hands steepled beneath his chin.

Rohmer began without further preamble.

"Dr. Fu-Manchu, who is the antagonist of my little midnight-crawler, is not entirely a creature of fiction. He is based upon a Chinese master criminal known only as 'Mr. King,' who was the principal supplier of opium to the Limehouse district of London at the time I was researching an article on the subject for a magazine. He was a shadowy figure, and though I heard his name whispered everywhere in China-town, I never laid eyes upon him until long after I had filed the story, when I chanced to glimpse him crossing the pavement from an automobile into a house.

"I had not even heard him so much as described, yet I knew on the instant it was he. He was as tall and dignified a celestial as you are ever likely to meet, attired in a fur cap and a long overcoat with a fur collar, followed closely by a stunningly beautiful Arab girl wrapped in a grey fur cloak. The girl was a dusky angel, in the company of a man whose face I can only describe as the living embodiment of Satan.

"That, gentlemen," he concluded quietly, "is Dr. Fu-Manchu, as I have come to present him in writing and to picture him in my nightmares."

"Who was the girl?" I heard myself asking; and inwardly jeered at myself for harbouring the interests of a young rake in the body of a sixty-one-year-old professional man.

Rohmer, who like Holmes was a pipe smoker, shrugged in the midst of scooping tobacco from an old leather pouch into a crusty brier. "His mistress, perhaps, or merely a transient. In any case I never saw her again."

Holmes intervened. "I take it by that statement that you did see Mr. King subsequent to that occasion."

"Not according to the information I gave to my publicist, or for that matter anyone else, including my wife." He struck a match off his bootheel and puffed the pipe into an orange glow, meeting Holmes's gaze. "But, yes."

"And has he anything to do with the parcel which you have brought?"

"Again, the answer is yes." His eyes did not stray to the bundle he had placed atop the deal table where our host had once conducted his chemical researches, now a repository for the daily post. My own gaze, connected as it was to a curious mind, was drawn there directly. The item was roughly the size of a teacake, wrapped in burlap and tied with a cord. My fingers itched for my old notebook.

"Mr. King is no slouch," said Rohmer, "and like Dr. Watson, recognised himself immediately when he read my description of Fu-Manchu. Beyond this fact, the opium lord and the good doctor have nothing in common. Vexed though he might have been by my little theft, I'm convinced that Dr. Watson would not stoop so far as to kidnap me and threaten my life."

"Good Lord!" I exclaimed. In my foolish complacency I had formed the fancy that such incidents had been left behind with the dead century.

Holmes's guest proceeded to exhibit his flair for narrative with a colourful but concise account of his recent adventure.

Whilst strolling the twisting streets of Limehouse in quest of literary inspiration recently, he had been seized and forced into a touring car by two dark-skinned brutes—Bedouins, he thought—in shaggy black beards and ill-fitting European dress, who conveyed him to that selfsame house before which he had first set eyes upon Mr. King. There, in a windowless room decorated only with an ancient Chinese tapestry upon one wall, he was left along with that weird Satanic creature, attired in a plain yellow robe and mandarin's cap, who interviewed him from behind a homely oak desk, enquiring about the source of his novel. In precise, unaccented English, Mr. King expressed particular interest in the character of Dr. Fu-Manchu, the wicked Chinese ascetic bent upon world domination by the East.

"He is a creature of my imagination," Rohmer had insisted; for he intuited that to profess otherwise would seal his doom.

"Pray do not insult me," Mr. King replied evenly. "I am a law-abiding British resident. Import-export is my trade, and I have no wish to conquer this troubled planet. Beyond these things, your description of me is accurate in every detail. Was it your purpose to malign my character?"

"It was not."

"And yet I find myself incapable of doing business with gentlemen who placed absolute faith in my integrity before your canard appeared. If the situation continues I shall face ruin."

"I sympathise. However, I am not responsible for your sour fortune."

"Will you withdraw the book from circulation?"

"I shan't. I am informed its sales are increasing."

Mr. King stroked his great brow.

"May I at least extract your word of honour that this ogre who resembles me will not be seen again once the novel is no longer in print?"

"You may not. I am writing a sequel."

"I could bring suit, of course. However, the courts take too long, and in the meantime I shall have no source of income. Shall I threaten you?"

"I rather wish you would. This conversation has become tedious."

At this point in Rohmer's account I laughed despite myself. Here was an Englishman! He continued without acknowledging the interruption.

Mr. King's devilish features assumed a saturnine arrangement, he informed us. "I am, as I said, respectful of your laws. This was not always the case. It is difficult for a Chinese to advance himself in business in this society; I was forced to take certain measures, the nature of which I shall not define. I assume you are aware that if you were never to leave this house, your body would never be recovered?"

Rohmer confided to Holmes and me that he had not been so sanguine as he'd pretended. He knew the house stood before a dock, and that many a weighted corpse lay on the bottom of the Thames with little hope of recovery. The thought that his wife should never learn of his true fate very nearly unmanned him. Yet he held his tongue.

"I shall accept your silence as an affirmative response," said the Chinese. "However, I am not without reason, and I am in the way of being a sporting man."

Hereupon he struck a miniature gong which stood upon the desk. It had scarcely finished reverberating when one of the villains who had abducted Rohmer, now draped in the burnoose and robes of the authentic Bedouin, entered through an opening hidden behind the tapestry, placed a singular object next to the gong, and withdrew.

"This bowl is said to have belonged to the Emperor Han, who ruled China from 206 until 220 A.D.," said Mr. King, lifting the ornate object. "Such things are priceless. I lend it to you, in the certainty that a clever fellow such as yourself will succeed in unlocking its riddle. If in Thursday's *Times* I read the answer in the personal columns, the bowl shall be yours, with my compliments. If upon that day the late edition has come and gone and no such item has appeared, you will not live an hour more. You have seen how easily my subordinates may lay hands upon your person. I believe you know I speak the truth."

Rohmer concluded his tale at the moment he finished his pipe. He laid it in his lap to cool.

"I accepted the bowl, for what else could I do? Mr. King then used the gong to summon the Bedouins, both of whom were again costumed as Occidentals, and they returned me to the spot where they had first accosted me. I went home, and puzzled over the thing the night through. Morning came and I was nowhere nearer the solution—indeed, to the nature of the riddle itself—than I was yesterday evening, so I sent you the message which resulted in your kind invitation. Tomorrow is Thursday. Can you help me, Mr. Holmes? It is for my wife I am concerned. I've cost her many a sleepless hour with my rash wanderings. To leave her a widow at her tender age would be a mortal sin."

"Your Mr. King is transparent, and hardly inscrutable," said Holmes. "He fears attention and investigation more than the loss of legitimate business, if the resume you supplied is reliable." He rubbed his hands in the way I remembered from long ago, signifying his eagerness to solve the problem which had been set before him—though he may merely have been massaging his joints. "You were correct to come to me rather than to the police. Scotland Yard teems with fresh new faces, behind which churn the same old brains. Let us examine this wondrous bowl."

Rohmer stood, retrieved the bundle he had brought, and placed it in Holmes's hands. A twitch of the cord, and the sun came into the room in the form of a beautiful thing which glistened as if still molten. I rose and bent over my friend, that I might see what he saw at the moment he saw it. It seemed that even in my extremity I remained the same curious creature I had been when I was no older than young Rohmer.

The workmanship was exquisite. The bowl was just large enough to hold in two hands, so bright and gleaming it might have been just struck off. Around the outside of the rim paraded a row of playful monkeys in relief, no two of which wore the same expression, and each so lifelike as to seem poised to leap from its perch and gambol about that staid room. There were thirteen in all, some crouching, some reclining upon their backs, others in the attitude of stalking, rumps in the air and noses nearly touching the ground. One, of more mischievous mien than all the rest, hung from its tail, the tail curling well above the bowl's rim, and stared straight out with arms crossed and lips peeled back into a jeering grin, as though daring the casual handler to unlock the riddle of the golden monkeys.

"This is formidable craftsmanship." Holmes studied the outside, the inside, then turned it over and scrutinised the bottom, which bore no mark. At length he proffered it to me. "What do you make of it, Watson? I confess chinoiserie is far from my long suit."

I hefted it. It weighed, I should have judged, nearly four pounds. "It is twenty-four karat, Holmes. I would stake my life upon it."

"Mr. Rohmer has already staked his. It seems scarcely large enough to support more than one." He took the bowl from me and charged his own pipe. "I commend to you both the sea air. Mind the bees. They are in a petulant humour this season."

I understood this to be a dismissal, and conducted the writer to the outdoors, where we strolled along the chalk cliff listening to the restless Channel coursing along the base. To our left, Holmes's bees swarmed about his city of hives, which reminded me so much of the mosques and minarets of Afghanistan.

"Mr. Holmes is older than I'd suspected," declared my companion. "Your accounts paint such a youthful and energetic picture that I suppose I thought he was immune to dissipation. Do you think his mental powers sufficient to this challenge?"

"The crown jewels reside in an ancient structure," I replied. "They shine now as they have for four hundred years."

"That is true." He sounded unconvinced.

We spent the remainder of our outing discussing Egypt, which Rohmer was eager to visit, and which I had known intimately long before any tourist with the wherewithal could hire a camel and have his likeness struck before the Sphinx. We took our rest upon a marble bench whilst he bombarded me with questions. When after two hours we returned to the villa, I was quite drained and looking forwards to a whisky-and-soda and silence; the latter a requisite during Holmes's deliberations.

Much to my surprise, we found him quite loquacious. He looked up with sparkling eyes through a veritable "London particular" of tobacco-smoke and bade us be seated. The floor about his feet was piled with books from his shelves, many of which were splayed open upon their spines or stood like tents on the carpet. I noted Lutz's *History of the Chinese Dynasties*, Walker's *Ancient Metalwork*, and Carroll's *World Primates* among the variety of titles. The wonderful golden bowl rested in his lap.

"Dr. Watson can attest that it is a long-held axiom of mine that one cannot make bricks without clay," Holmes informed Rohmer, who unlike me had declined an invitation to make free with the siphon and bottle. "I am to some degree an autodidact, and most of my education regarding arcane subjects has taken place in the pursuit of the solution to problems which at first appeared puerile. When we met, I astounded Watson with the announcement that I was unaware of Copernicus or his theories; however, I have since qualified as an expert. At the end of two hours, the lost-wax process is not lost to me. Similarly, I may converse with some authority upon the Emperor Han's propensity towards painful boils, the origin of the Troy ounce, and some indelicacies in the matter of the posteriors of certain species of gibbon. I am enormously wealthier for the time spent."

"But is my wife any less likely to suffer bereavement?" Rohmer's tone was impatient. He had evidently concluded that Holmes's remarkable mind had commenced to wander. It shames me to confess that I harboured similar doubts. Professor Moriarty and his equally perfidious minion Colonel Moran had been mouldering now for nearly a quarter-century, and time was scarcely more kind to the faculties of reason.

"That I cannot say," Holmes declared.

Rohmer's face fell.

"The future is a closed book, even to me," continued the retired detective. "For all I am aware, your driver may become distracted on the way back to Newhaven and precipitate you both over the cliff. However, assuming that your Mr. King is a man of his word, Mrs. Rohmer will not grieve because the golden monkeys have refused to give up their secret. The riddle is solved."

The young are easily read. I saw hope and relief and a dark shadow of doubt upon the writer's face. He leaned forwards to hear Holmes's explanation, Holmes leaned forwards to provide it. Those two hawklike profiles in such close proximity gave me the fancy that Rohmer was gazing into a somewhat clouded mirror.

"I began with the obvious, an examination of the bowl for a hidden recess, containing some item of interest: The term 'Chinese box' is founded in reality. The metal is seamless, made no hollow sound when I tapped it all over, and none of the graven images performed double duty as a release mechanism. In any event, so unimaginative a solution would have disappointed me, given your impression of Mr. King's intellect. I call your attention to the design. Doesn't it strike you as remarkable?"

His guest accepted the return of the artifact and rotated it slowly, scowling in deep concentration. "It's a masterpiece, certainly. To think that the Chinese were executing such things when we English were living in mud huts makes one wonder why they do not already rule the world."

"Just so. However, that is material for another conversation, one which will almost certainly not involve this particular piece." Having made this cryptic pronouncement, Holmes plunged ahead without pause. "I direct your young eyes towards the monkeys themselves. Does any of them stand out from the crowd?"

"They are all so lifelike. The one with its arms folded has claimed my attention from the start. The cheeky little fellow seems just this side of thrusting out his tongue."

"Devilishly clever, these Chinese," said Holmes. "It could be a diversionary tactic to lure the casual observer away from something more informative. Not in this case, however. What do you know of monkeys?"

His guest sought his answer in the ceiling. "According to Professor Darwin, they are related to you and me, and the Americans are of the opinion that they are quite amusing by the barrel. I know a bit more about marmosets, but none is represented here. I'm afraid that's the sum total of my knowledge as regards the species."

"Perhaps you will find Mr. Carroll of assistance." Holmes scooped up *World Primates* and presented it with his thumb marking the place to which it had lain open. "I would now direct your eye to the passage I have underlined."

Rohmer carefully laid the precious bowl beside him on the divan and accepted the book. He read aloud:

"'Monkeys occupy two separate and distinct groups, one native to the Old World, the other to the New, in particular Central and South America. Old World monkeys are characterised by their narrow probosci, and are referred to as Catarrhine; none possesses a prehensile tail. Their American cousins are recognised by their flat probosci, and these are designated Platyrrhine; their tails are prehensile.'"

The young man closed the book, picked up the bowl once again, and studied each of the golden monkeys in turn. "All the noses appear similar. I believe they are flat, but lacking the other variety for purposes of comparison, I cannot say definitely. How narrow is narrow?"

"A valid observation. As Aristotle said in another context, one requires a place to stand. Disregard, then, the question of monkeys' noses. What do you make of this business of tails?"

"Merely that Old World monkeys are incapable of swinging or hanging by them, while those from the New . . ." Rohmer's voice trailed off. He was staring at the insolent primate with arms folded and tail curled over the lip of the bowl. "Great heavens! And I presume to call myself an Orientalist."

"It is a broad subject. No one man can claim to know it in its entirety. The Chinese were among the first to discover the African continent and to study its flora and fauna. They were privileged to incorporate African motifs into their art. However, for all its advances, even that estimable society could not, in the third century A.D., posit a monkey hanging by its tail twelve hundred years before the discovery of the one continent whose simian population was thus capable.

"The bowl is a forgery," Holmes concluded. "There is the answer to your riddle."

"Great heavens!" I exclaimed, at the moment unaware that I had echoed Rohmer's words.

Once again, Holmes's guest presented a study in conflicting emotions: Relief, wonder, and disappointment paraded across his face in a variety nearly as rich as that provided by the golden monkeys. "When did you suspect?"

"At the moment the bowl appeared in your narrative. It did not seem likely that Mr. King would threaten you in one breath and in the next offer you an item so tantalising without some promise of benefit to himself. The same rules that govern legitimate commerce also apply to the *demimonde*.

"At first, of course, I had to eliminate the mundane possibility of a niche concealed in the bowl. That attended to, the crucial factor was the character of the enemy. It was not enough to this fellow that you should fear for your life; should you manage to uncover the secret, the solution itself must rob your triumph of its savour. Remember that Mr. King represents a culture that has had two thousand years to refine the punishment of torture. Armed with that intelligence, I proceeded on the assumption that the bowl was counterfeit. Any reputable dealer in antiquities could have done the rest."

"Then the thing is worthless." Rohmer gazed disconsolately at the object in his hands.

"Not quite," said Holmes. "Although I should be much surprised if upon scratching it you do not discover base lead beneath the plate. The workmanship is still a thing of beauty. A London pawnbroker might be persuaded to part with ten pounds in order to display it in his shop window."

"Still, I have been cheated. That fraudulent old devil led me to believe I would own something of real value."

"But you do. He has given you the gift of your life."

Somewhere in the villa a clock chimed the hour. Holmes stirred. "There is a telephone in the hall, which you may use to order an auto to return you to the station. First, however, I suggest you ring up the *Times* and place an advertisement announcing the riddle's solution in tomorrow's edition."

Sax Rohmer regarded Sherlock Holmes with an expression I had seen many times upon many faces. "You are still the best detective in England."

"Thank you." Holmes closed his eyes, displaying for the first time the weariness which his feat of brilliance had created; he was, when all was said and done, a man in the sixtieth year of an adventurous life sufficient for ten of his contemporaries. "One never tires of hearing it," said he.

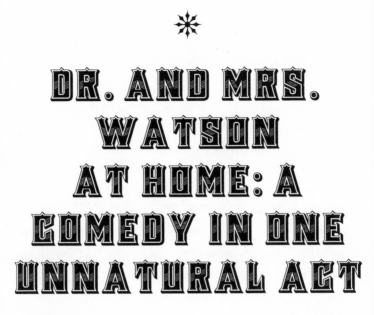

DR. AND MRS. WATSON AT HOME: A COMEDY IN ONE UNNATURAL ACT

uthor's Note: I wrote "Dr. and Mrs. Watson at Home" to be performed by a two-person cast for my fellow members of The Arcadia Mixture, the Ann Arbor, Michigan, scion of the national Baker Street Irregulars. Although casual readers of Holmes may find some of its lighthearted references a bit "inside" (not to say somewhat corny), diehard Sherlockians may appreciate the shout-out. Both may agree that the Mrs. Watson in the original stories always seemed a bit too understanding about her husband's frequent desertions of her to gad about with his former roommate.

TIME: 1890-ish

SCENE: The sitting-room of JOHN H. and MARY MORSTAN WATSON's London home. MARY is busy knitting.

MARY. *Knit one, purl two. Or is it purl two, knit one? What's the difference, anyway? Ever since those buffoons lost the Agra treasure, the closest I've come to real pearls is an occasional oyster at Simpson's. (Knits some more in silence.) What an elaborate waste of a Victorian lady's time. It wouldn't be so bad if I knew how to knit something besides mufflers. I'll bet if you laid all the mufflers I've made end to end they'd reach twice round London. Or once round Mycroft Holmes's neck. Boring! There's only one thing I can think of that's more tedious than a muffler.*

WATSON *enters, pecks MARY on the cheek.*

WATSON. *Hello, lambchop.*

MARY *(without enthusiasm). Hello, James.*

WATSON. *John. My name's John.*

MARY. *Oh, yes; I keep forgetting.*

WATSON. *Why is it that after three years of marriage you still call me James?*

MARY. *Can I help it if I get mixed up? Everyone you do business with is named James: James Phillimore, James Mortimer, James Lancaster, all three Moriarty brothers—*

WATSON *(looking around quickly). Moriarty? Where? Where?*

MARY. *Oh, calm down. He's not here. I swear, you've a fixation about that poor man every bit as bad as your friend Sherlock Holmes's.*

WATSON. *Poor? Professor Moriarty? The Napoleon of Crime? The most dangerous man in London? The organizer of half that is criminal and of nearly all that is undetected in this city?*

MARY. *That's exactly what I mean. How's the fellow to make anything of himself if all everyone does is criticise?*

WATSON *(massaging his temples). Don't start, Mary. I've had a trying day. It's murder being around sick people all the time.*

MARY. *Why'd you become a doctor then?*

WATSON. *The ceramics class was full. What's for supper?*

MARY. *Woodcock.*

WATSON. *Damn.*

MARY. *What's wrong with woodcock?*

WATSON. *I had it for lunch.*

MARY. *You've been eating with Sherlock Holmes again, haven't you?*

WATSON. *How did you know?*

MARY. *Elementary, my dear dum-dum. Woodcock is the only thing Holmes eats.*

WATSON. *That's not true. Just last Christmas Peterson, the Commissionaire, gave him a goose.*

MARY. *I've always wondered about him.*

WATSON *(thoughtfully). He does fuss a lot with his uniform.*

MARY. *I'm talking about Holmes, not Peterson.*

WATSON. *Holmes! How can you say that about the best and wisest man I've ever known? Are you forgetting that if it weren't for him you and I would never have met?*

MARY *(dryly). That's hardly a point in his favour.*

WATSON. *If you're bored with me, I suggest you get a job. I understand there's an opening at the Copper Beeches.*

MARY. *Funny. What's the Great Detective up to this time? Counting orange pips?*

WATSON. *He was deciphering a palimpsest, whatever that is. And staring at a lot of dancing men.*

MARY (*smugly*). *What did I tell you?*

WATSON. *No, no. It's a cipher of some kind. Has to do with a fellow and his wife out in Norfolk. I must say it's too deep for me.*

MARY. *McGuffey's Reader would be too deep for you.*

WATSON (*impatient*). *Isn't it time you visited your mother?*

MARY. *My mother's dead. Now who's forgetting? You talk just like you write.*

WATSON. *Let my writing alone. It pays the bills, doesn't it?*

MARY. *Something has to.*

WATSON. *What is that supposed to mean?*

MARY. *Let's face it, James—*

WATSON. *John. My name's John.*

MARY. *Whatever. The Speckled Band couldn't live on what you make off that crummy practice of yours.*

WATSON. *You knew what I was when you married me. Whoever heard of a rich doctor?*

MARY. *Anstruther does all right. He bought his wife a fur coat for her birthday. And you know why he can afford it, don't you?*

WATSON. *Don't start, Mary.*

MARY. *He can afford it because you keep turning over your patients to him so you can run off and do God-knows-what with your friend Sherlock Holmes.*

WATSON. *You're starting.*

MARY. *And how does Holmes show his appreciation? By treating you like a servant. Has he ever once offered to share with you his reward for solving a mystery?*

WATSON. *What about that gift he gave us last Christmas?*

MARY. *Hallelujah! A six-karat gold snuffbox with an amethyst on the lid. Talk about your bad taste!*

WATSON. *I happen to think it's beautiful. Anyway, Holmes wouldn't insult me by offering me money.*

MARY. *He could be discourteous now and then.*

(There's a knock at the door.)

WATSON. *I'll get it. (exits)*

MARY *(knitting). I hope it's Jack the Ripper making a house call.*

WATSON *(re-entering, carrying a fold of paper). It was a messenger.*

MARY. *Did you tip him?*

WATSON. *I couldn't. There's no cash in the house and I left my cheque-book in Holmes's desk.*

MARY. *That's what you told the last messenger. Pretty soon they'll catch on.*

WATSON *(unfolding the paper). It's from Holmes.*

MARY. *Just as I thought. Junk mail.*

WATSON. *He needs me, Mary. He's on something.*

MARY. *When isn't he?*

WATSON. *I must go to him. Where is my trusty revolver?*

MARY. *In the top drawer of the bureau, under your faithful socks.*

WATSON. *Forget it. No time. I'll borrow Holmes's hair-trigger.*

MARY. *Don't tell me that mangy animal has started up again out at the Baskervilles'. Why can't they call the dogcatcher like everyone else?*

WATSON. *I'll explain later. (pecks her on the cheek) Don't wait up for me. I may be late.*

MARY *(coldly). Who is it this time, Violet Hunter or that Ferguson tramp?*

WATSON. *What are you talking about?*

MARY. *You know very well what. Holmes, ha! The last time you said he needed you, you came back with a long brown hair on your coat.*

WATSON. *I told you that hair belonged to an ichneumon!*

MARY. *I don't care what her nationality was. If you don't stop seeing other women, I'll leave you. Put that in your cherrywood and smoke it!*

WATSON. *We'll talk about this later.*

MARY. *We most certainly will, James.*

WATSON. *John. My name's John.*

MARY. *Whatever!*

(WATSON exits. MARY continues knitting a moment longer, then straightens in the attitude of listening. Satisfied her husband has left, she picks up the telephone, rattles the fork.)

MARY. *Professor Moriarty, please. (waits) Hello, Jimmy? Mary. He's gone. No, he won't be home until late. Are you free tonight? Wonderful. What? (pause) New monograph? Yes, bring it along, by all means. (coquettishly) Yes, I'd love to discuss the dynamics of your asteroid. I'm counting the minutes. Goodbye, love. (hangs up)*

CURTAIN.

THE ADVENTURE OF THE COUGHING DENTIST

hroughout the first year of our association, Mr. Sherlock Holmes and I were rather like strangers wed by prearrangement: mutually respectful, but uncertain of the person with whom each was sharing accommodations. The situation was ungainly, to say the least, because upon the surface we were very different individuals indeed. When, therefore, it chanced that we should travel together abroad, we agreed without hesitation. As Mr. Clemens says (mortally assaulting the Queen's English), "I have found that there ain't no better way to find out whether you like people or hate them than to travel with them."

As it happened, both Scotland Yard and the *Times* of London, which was publishing a series chronicling the tragic events I have set down elsewhere under the somewhat sensational title of *A Study in Scarlet*, had asked Holmes to visit the place where the troubles involving Enoch Drebber, Joseph Stangerson, and Jefferson Hope had begun, and apply his formidable detecting skills towards eliminating a number of small discrepancies in the murderer's confession. This journey, with expenses to be paid by the *Times* in return for an exclusive report of the investigation, would take us to Salt Lake City, the capital of Mormon country in the Utah Territory, a strange and terrible place not unlike Afghanistan of darkest memory.

When I say that we did not hesitate to accept the offer, I do not mean to imply that we failed to discuss it at length in the privacy of our Baker Street digs.

"This is redolent of inspectors Gregson and Lestrade," said Holmes, flicking his long tapering fingers at the telegram from the *Times* as he lounged in his basket chair. "They were swift to claim credit when the boat seemed seaworthy, but now that it's sprung a leak or two they seek to abandon ship and let me go down with it."

"Undoubtedly. But if you're still certain of the soundness of the solution—"

"I'd stake my reputation upon it, were I to possess such a thing."

"Then," said I, "you have nothing to lose but a month or so from your studies here, and a holiday to gain."

"Holidays are for the overworked. I am singularly idle thanks to my magnanimity towards the Yard. The press perceived it to be a police case from start to finish until this moment." He made a motion of dismissal, exactly as if he were slashing his bow across the strings of his violin. Then his face assumed a quizzical expression. "You say 'you' as if I am to be alone in this excursion. What do I know of being a special correspondent? You're the literary half of this partnership, Doctor."

"That's flattering, but premature. I've only just begun arranging my notes, and there is no guarantee of publication, rather the opposite. I'm just one more returning veteran with a story to tell. Fleet Street must be crowded to the rafters with unrequested and unwelcome manuscripts like mine."

"Hardly like yours. There's romance in the business, murder, and not a line about troop movements or grand strategy. I'd read it myself if I didn't know the ending already. I never accept a pig without a poke. No, Doctor, I shan't undertake the assignment without a companion upon whose loyalty and discretion I can rely without question. What is your answer?"

"I was afraid you'd never ask."

His smile was shy, an emotion I had thought absent from his meagre repertoire. We would be quite on the other side of our second adventure before such reticence vanished from our relationship forever.

Our crossing was not uneventful, despite calm seas; but the affair of the American industrialist and the Swedish stowaway presents facets of its own, and its appearance in these pages would only distract the reader from the circumstances I am about to relate. It is a story the world may be prepared to hear, but which I am unprepared to tell. As many times as Holmes has explained to me how a disparity between a ship's bells and the time on a pocket watch, *both equally accurate*, can coexist, I remain ignorant as to how he brought the matter to a satisfactory conclusion before we arrived in the Port of New York.

Ironically, the very questions that brought us from our hemisphere and across the vast reaches of the North American continent proved easier to answer than the conundrum aboard ship. Suffice it to say that a minor but crucial player in the Hope tragedy lied to dissemble a sordid personal peccadillo, and that most of the burden fell to me as I struggled to turn a half-penny hurricane into four columns in the *Times*. They were printed, and our fare and lodgings were paid for without complaint, but from that day to this I have not received an invitation to submit so much as a line to that august institution.

Our mission completed, we were left with a wealth of time and opportunity to broaden our experience of the world's curiosities. I circumnavigated the gargantuan lake in a hired launch, and Holmes made copious entries in his notebook about the practice of polygamy for a monograph upon the subject, but we were both still eager to add to our education, and were soon off to Denver.

On the way, we were detained in a muddy little hamlet whose police force had been forewarned of a visit by the remnants of the Jesse James gang of notorious reputation, suspected because of our British accents and European clothes as bandits in disguise. While awaiting word from Washington, D.C., confirming the material in our travel documents, we were placed under house arrest in the town's only hotel. One of our guards was a friendly fellow with swooping moustaches and a revolver the size of a meat-axe, who taught us the rudiments of the game of Faro. By the time we were released, Holmes had become an expert, and I had learned just enough to swear off playing ever again for the sake of my army pension.

Having lost several days, we elected to forego Denver as just another large city like St. Louis, and turned south towards the Territory of Arizona. There among weird rock formations and cactus plants shaped like tall men with arms upraised, I remarked to my companion that I was disappointed not to have seen a red Indian yet, to add to my observations of the aborigines upon three continents.

"In order to make an observation, one must first observe," said Holmes. "Those silhouettes are not the product of erosion."

I followed the direction of his pointing finger, but we had nearly drawn beyond range before I identified what looked like broken battlements atop a sandstone ridge as a group of motionless horsemen watching the train steam past.

"Apaches, if my preliminary reading is accurate. Zulus are peace lovers by comparison." He laid aside his *Rocky Mountain News* and uncocked the Eley's pistol he was holding in his lap.

"You might have said something. I'm no babe in the woods, you know."

"Quite the opposite, Doctor. A seasoned warrior like yourself might have responded from instinct and training. That would in all likelihood precipitate an action we should all regret."

"I am not a hothead." I fear I sounded petulant.

"You've given me no reason to think otherwise. Now that you have so informed me, as one gentleman to another, I shall not repeat the mistake."

Ours was a difficult getting-acquainted period, as I've said. Even my dear late wife and I had an easier time of it; but then I'd had the advantage of having saved her life early in the courtship. I can't recommend a better approach when it comes to breaking the ice.

The gypsy life deposited us at length in the city of Youngblood, some forty miles north of Tucson. I'm told the place no longer exists, with nary a broken bottle nor a stone standing upon stone to indicate it ever did. I do not grieve over this pass.

Why we alighted in this vagabond jungle of canvas and clapboard, with an open sewer running merrily down its main street, is a question I cannot answer with certainty. We had not paused thirty seconds to take on water when Holmes shot to his feet and snatched his Gladstone bag from the brass rack overhead. Perhaps it was the scenery which inspired him. I vividly recall a one-eyed mongrel performing its ablutions on the platform and an ancient red Indian wrapped in a filthy blanket attempting to peddle an earthenware pot to everyone who stepped down from the train. A place so sinister in appearance seemed an ideal location for a consulting detective to practise his trade; then again, he may simply have been drawn to its perfect ugliness through some aesthetic of his own.

"Well, Doctor?" He stood in the aisle holding out my medical bag. His eyes glittered.

"Here?"

"Here forsooth. Can you picture a place further removed from Mayfair?"

For this I could offer no argument, and so I took the bag and hoisted my army footlocker from the rack.

Approaching the exit, Holmes nearly collided with a man boarding. When Holmes asked his pardon, the fellow started and seized him by the shoulders.

"There's no call, stranger, if that accent's real and it belongs to Sherlock Holmes."

The reader will indulge me if I remind him that at this juncture in his long and illustrious career, my companion was no more public a figure than the thousands of immigrants then pouring into the frontier in pursuit of free land, precious metal for the taking, and the promise of a new life. To hear one's associate addressed by name so far from home was as much a surprise as to be struck by a bullet on some peaceful corner, and one nearly as unsettling. My hand went to the revolver in my pocket.

"I believe you have the advantage," said Holmes stiffly.

He did indeed. The stranger was as tall as my fellow lodger, and a distinct specimen of the Western type, with long fair hair, splendid moustaches, and a strong-jowled face deeply tanned despite the broad brim of his black hat. He wore a Prince Albert coat of the same funereal hue over a gaily printed waistcoat, striped trousers stuffed into the tops of tall black boots, and a revolver every bit as large as our erstwhile jailer's on his hip. I left my much smaller weapon in its pocket—albeit gripping it tightly—in the sudden certainty that any swift move by me would be met by one considerably swifter on his part, and far more deadly.

To my surprise, the man released his grip upon Holmes's shoulders and stepped back, dipping his head in a show of deference. "No offence meant. I feared I'd missed you, and charging square into you like a bull buffalo set my good manners clear to rout. Wyatt Earp, sir, late of Tombstone, and headed I-don't-know-where, or was anyway till I set foot in this hell."

The name signified nothing to me and was so unusual that I took it at first as a statement interrupted by gastric distress: "Why, at—urp!" was how I received his introduction. Having sampled in Colorado the popular regional fare of beans and hot peppers stewed and served in a bowl, I had been suffering from the same complaint for several hundreds of miles.

Holmes did not share this delusion, and he, who in later years would treat kings and supercriminals with the same cordial disdain, became deferential on the instant.

"I am just off reading of your exploits in the *Rocky Mountain News*. This business in a certain corral—"

"It wasn't in the O.K., but in an alley down the street next to the photo studio of C.S. Fly; but I don't reckon 'The Shoot-out in Fly's Alley' would make it as far as Denver. It cost me a brother last March, and crippled another one three months before that. I'm not finished collecting on that bill, but it's not why I met this train. I saw a piece about you being in jail up north—"

It was Holmes's turn to interrupt.

"Hardly a jail, although the condition of the hotel was a crime in itself. I'm curious as to the process by which you deduced I would proceed south from there, instead of east to Denver."

"You're a detective, the piece said, vacationing from England. I'm in sort of that line myself, tracking stagecoach robbers and such, and it occurred to me nobody who's truly interested in crime and them that commit it would bother with a place where there's a policeman on every corner. I wouldn't give a spruce nickel for a blue-tick hound that didn't head straight for the brambles."

"The brambles in this case being Arizona, where the savages don't all wear paint and feathers," Holmes said. "It's crude reasoning, filled with flaws, but I warrant that within six months you'd make chief inspector at Scotland Yard." He shook the stranger's hand firmly. "My associate, Dr. John H. Watson."

The sun broke in the man's features. "Doc, is it? Well, if that's not a good show card, I'll give up the game."

I accepted the grip of Mr. Wyatt Earp, late of Tombstone. When winters are damp, I still feel it in my fingers.

"I'm glad to see you travelling with a friend." Earp sipped from his glass of beer, which after thirty minutes was not half gone; he seemed a man who kept his appetites tightly in rein. "I don't know how things are in England, though I expect they've settled a bit since Shakespeare, but no matter how much attention a man pays to his cuffs and flatware, he needs a good man at his back."

Holmes said, "Dr. Watson is my Sancho Panza. You would have marvelled to see his stone face just before I clapped the irons on Jefferson Hope."

We were relaxing in the cool dry shade of the Mescalero Saloon, a model of the rustic American public house, with a long carved mahogany bar standing in sharp contrast to the rough plank floor, cuspidors in an execrable state of maintenance, and the head of an enormous grizzly bear mounted on a wall flanked by portraits of the martyred presidents Abraham Lincoln and James A. Garfield. Some marksman, possibly of a patriotic bent, had managed to put out one of the grizzly's eyes and its left canine without nicking either commander-in-chief. I felt distinctly out of my element, and ordered a third whisky-and-water. Our new acquaintance's tales of romance and gunplay in Dodge City and else-where required stimulants to digest. I was unclear as to whether he was a gambler or a road agent or a peace officer or a liar on the grand scale of P. T. Barnum. As a frustrated writer, I itched to commit his stories to paper, but as a man of science, I thought him a charlatan.

"I'm ignorant as to Hopes, but I pride myself on my Cervantes," said Earp. "My father wanted me to practise law."

"The errors of la Mancha and Richard III are most instructive in the legal profession." Holmes drank beer. I had the impression that among Mongols he'd have slaked his thirst with mare's milk. I never knew a man who assimilated himself so thoroughly with the natives. "However, we have not come to this place to discuss the classics."

Earp seemed to concentrate upon lighting a cigar, but it seemed to me all his attention was on Holmes.

"They're set on hanging my friend. I don't mind telling you I'm against it."

Holmes's eyes glittered. Direct speech affected him like a chemical stimulant. "Dr. John Henry Holliday."

"I see you're a man who squeezes all the juice he can out of a newspaper. If you know his name, you know I'd never have walked out of that alley but for Doc. He killed two men who wanted me in hell, both in the space of a half minute."

"And he calls himself a physician! What about his oath?" My exposure to war had not prepared me for barbarism in the humanitarian professions.

Earp's reptilian gaze was uncannily like Holmes's when he placed me under scrutiny.

"Doc's a dentist, if it counts. He's separated more men from their teeth than their lives, but that was before consumption got the better of him. He came out from Georgia for his health. It don't look like the locals mean for him to find it."

He explained that he and "Doc" Holliday had left Tombstone to seek out and confront the conspirators who had slain Earp's brother Morgan and severely wounded Virgil, another brother. The precise cause of these attacks, and of the murderous street fight that had preceded them, was shrouded in territorial politics I could not understand. I gathered that this mission of vengeance had succeeded to some extent, but that Holliday had suffered a relapse of his corrosive pulmonary disease and come to Youngblood for medical attention. When after a few days his friend arrived to look in on him, he found him in jail charged with murder.

"It happened last night; I just missed it. Doc don't make friends easy, but he draws enemies like flies to sorghum. They say he disagreed with a tin-panner over the proper number of aces in a deck. The tin-panner knocked him down, which you can do with a finger when Doc's ailing. They say Doc gunned him in front of a gang of witnesses down the hill an hour or so later."

"Is he guilty?" Holmes asked.

"He says he's not sure. He took a bottle back to his room after he got up from the floor and don't remember a thing till the town marshal pulled him out of bed and threw him in a cell."

Holmes asked if he'd been convicted.

"The town's just a mining camp with no authority. They can't hold a trial till the circuit judge gets here. That could take days or months, and these get-rich-now prospectors aren't inclined to be patient. Hank Littlejohn was well-liked by all but three, and the other two didn't dislike him enough to go up against a bunch of tin-panners with guns and a rope over the likes of Doc. I ask you now, does that look like a party that'd sit on its hands when hemp's so cheap?" He inclined his head towards a group of men in muddy overalls hunched at the end of the bar, drinking straight whisky and taking turns looking over their shoulders towards our table.

Holmes kept his eyes on Earp. "I noticed them when they came in. The former teamster is their leader. He is the only one who hasn't looked our way."

"What makes him a teamster?" Earp asked. "They all look the same in them Tombstone tuxedoes."

"Such muscular development as his is a common result of swinging a pickaxe or handling a team of mules or oxen. Since by calling them 'tin-panners' you suggest they haven't yet advanced beyond the stage of panning streams for nuggets, I must conclude they are not 'hardrock' miners. That serpentine scar coiled round his neck ending at the corner of his jaw could only be the consequence of an accident with a whip—a hazard of the trade, based upon my observations since St. Louis. 'Bull-whackers,' I believe the men are sometimes called."

"You're a detective, for a fact. I'm glad to see the scribblers got it right for once. That's Elmer Dundy, Hank Littlejohn's old partner. When they got here, they quit the freighting business to find their fortune in the hills."

"Holmes, he's coming this way." I slid my hand into my pocket.

"Hold, Doctor. We can't shoot them all."

Elmer Dundy was burned the color of the native sandstone, with a great bald head sunk between shoulders built for a yoke. His eyes were tiny black pebbles above a broken nose and a thick lower lip that sagged to show a row of brown teeth and green gums. He'd been drinking whisky from a beer glass, which he held by its handle in a fist the size of a mutton roast.

"So you dug up some friends," he told Earp in a Londonderry brogue—filtered, it seemed, through cactus spines. "They don't look like the killers you run with regular. What's the matter, they all fly the coop?"

Holmes intervened.

"You'll pardon my speaking without invitation, but I'm unaccustomed to being discussed in the third person when I am present. If you wish to address a question to myself or my companion, be kind enough to do so directly."

Dundy regarded the speaker. Holmes was stretched languidly in his chair with one arm slung over the back and his stick resting alongside his legs, crossed at the ankles.

"English!" The former teamster spat viciously, splattering the floor an inch from Holmes's boot, and swung the heavy beer glass at his head.

What happened then took place in less time than I can describe it.

Holmes seemed merely to shift his grip on the handle of his stick, the ferrule end flashed so swiftly it was a blur, and dropping one shoulder and twisting the handle slightly, he inserted the stick between the oaf's ankles and sent him crashing to the floor.

Only when the building shook beneath his impact did I claw out my weapon, but before I had it free, Wyatt Earp scooped out his enormous revolver, thumbing back the hammer and levelling the barrel at Dundy's friends, stopping them in mid-charge.

Belatedly, as it seemed, Dundy's thick beer glass, released as he fell, struck the floor with a thump. The gaggle of miners stared at it comically.

"Drag him out before he gives the place a bad name." Earp's tone was as hard and cold as steel.

"Wait."

I got up to examine the insensate man. I asked the bartender for brandy. That fellow had come round from behind the bar with a length of billiard cue in his fist, only to find the drama ended.

"Busthead's all I got," he growled.

I looked to Earp for a translation, but it was Holmes who supplied it.

"Whisky, in the regional argot; I'm assembling a glossary. The term may be ironic in the current context, but the spirits should prove more than strong enough, though the flesh be weak."

The remedy was produced—"Bill it to Dundy, when he's perpendicular," Earp instructed the bartender—and in a little while we were quit of the miners, who needed no further encouragement to conduct their unsteady friend outside.

Earp shook his head.

"I must tell Doc. Your partner's slow on the draw, but I doubt even Doc would think to pull a bad tooth from a man I buffaloed. I'd hire you both in a minute, but apart from my interest in the Faro game here in the Mescalero, I haven't a cartwheel dollar to pay you for your trouble. My luck's gone sour since the fight at Fly's."

Holmes finished his beer at a draught.

"I shall play you for my fee when the thing's done, and accept your promise of payment should I win. When may I speak with Holliday?"

We placed our bags in the bartender's charge, with a warning from Earp to look after them as if they were his own, and repaired to the jail.

The town's only building of substance was constructed of stone round an iron cage transported from some wild railhead that had been dismantled the last time the tracks moved westward; American civilisation, I learned, was a portable thing in that rapidly developing wilderness.

A gimlet-eyed deputy bit down upon Holmes's pound sterling, inspected the result, and gave us five minutes with the prisoner.

I have remarked frequently upon the ascetic gauntness of Sherlock Holmes, but he appeared well-fed in comparison with Dr. John Henry Holliday. Holliday was an exemplar of the attenuated Southern aristocrat, saffron in colour, with the skull plain under a crown of pale thinning hair and a lank set of imperials blurred by days without a razor. He sat in a six-by-eight-foot enclosure on a cot, with a deck of sweaty pasteboards laid out on the blanket in a game of patience. A dirty collarless shirt, wrinkled trousers with the braces dangling, and filthy stockings, all of good quality notwithstanding, comprised his entire costume.

"I detest this game," he said in lieu of salutation. "It's like making love to a mirror, with the prospect of humiliating yourself through failure."

"If it's the latter you wish to avoid, I should move the queen of clubs from the king of spades to the king of hearts. Unless, that is, black-on-black is the custom in this country."

The prisoner corrected the error with a throaty noise of self-disgust that turned into a paroxysm of coughing. He stifled it against a sleeve, which bore away with it a pink stain. His gaze, bright and bloodshot, took in Holmes.

"God's wounds, an Englishman. Is business so good we're importing hangmen now?"

Wyatt made introductions. Holmes began his interrogation before Holliday could form another ironic comment.

"Your friend said Hank Littlejohn was well-regarded among all but three. Who, pray, are the other two?"

"Algernon Woods and Jasper Riley. Woods stopped playing poker with Hank for the same reason I did, and Riley got into a dust-up with him on the road here over a sporting woman they both admired in Bisbee; but I wouldn't waste my time trying to pin it on either one." He coughed and turned up another card.

"Are their alibis so sound?"

"Jasper's is. The Chinaman who runs the opium concession here swears he was in his establishment smoking up dreams the night Hank got it. Being a celestial, he's got no friends in town and no reason to lie."

"Lies don't always need reasons. What about Woods?"

"Algernon says he was working late in his shop alone. He's not your man, or even half of him. He's a dwarf, and fat besides. No one would mistake him for me even on a dark night, and there was a moon out big as a pumpkin."

"You said he has a shop. He is a merchant?"

"He's a combination tailor and undertaker. I was his customer once and it looks like I will be again."

"Where were you when Littlejohn met his fate?"

"Sleeping off a drunk in Mrs. Blake's boardinghouse. Whisky's a thief of recollection, but I'm inclined towards that conclusion. If I was to start killing poker cheats, I'd never be quit of it, and I'm a lazy man."

"Thank you. Dr. Watson and I will do what can be done."

Holliday chuckled, coughed, placed a red ten on a black knave.

"I'd get to it directly. There's another big moon tonight, dandy for trimming trees with dentists."

"I cannot understand such a man," said I, when we were outside the jail.

Wyatt Earp dropped his cigar and crushed it under his heel. "You get used to that honey-and-molasses drawl. The Wester he goes, the Souther he gets."

"I was referring to his character. My training tells me he's a consumptive in the tertiary stage, but that's hardly a reason to joke about hanging."

"Life's a joke to Doc. What part of it he's got left is too small to take serious."

"It's not so small to you, however," Holmes observed.

"Nor mine to him neither, comes to that. He's innocent."

"Of that I have no doubt. A man who's so willing to accept death would sooner lie and say he's guilty."

"It'd stick in his craw."

"Let us see if this Chinese opium seller suffers from that condition. There is no such thing as a watertight boat or an ironclad alibi."

Earp led us to a large tent pitched upon a slope so steep it would flood during rains and collapse before a mild rockslide. The moss growing upon it made the interior as dark as a cave, lit only by greasy lanterns suspended above rows of folding campaign cots, some occupied by men mostly insensible. Evil smoke fouled the air. Earp slid his bandanna over his nose and mouth whilst I buried mine in my handkerchief. Holmes, meanwhile, took in a deep breath and let it out with a contented sigh.

"Wantee pipee?"

This invitation came from an Oriental in a black silk robe and mandarin's cap, round as Buddha and no taller than a child, albeit plainly in his sunset years. Gold shone in a wicked smile.

"No wantee pipee. Wantee straight talk, and not in pidgin. I know an Oxford accent when I hear it." Holmes held up a gold sovereign, snatching it back when a yellow claw snatched at it.

The old man shrugged and folded his hands inside the sleeves of his robe.

"The missionary who taught me was a retired don. If you are here on behalf of a wife or mother, you may browse among these wretches for him who is lost. I do not insist upon introductions and so am ignorant as to their names."

"If that is the case, how were you able to identify Jasper Riley among your customers the night Hank Littlejohn was killed?"

"I did not say I never pay attention to faces. In election years, many of my former colleagues in San Francisco went to jail because they failed to recognise the same undercover policemen who had arrested them before."

"Did Riley pay you to say he was here all night?"

"Had he been here and made the proper offer, I should have accepted; but honestly, do you think a common teamster could meet my fee for such a risk? I bring in more in a night than he sees in a month, and it is nothing to hang a Chinese here."

"Very well. Here is your sovereign."

The old man left his hands folded. "That is not the coin you showed me. You are not the magician you fancy yourself."

Holmes grunted as if put out, slipped the coin into his waistcoat pocket, and produced another from inside his cuff. This the opium seller took with a mocking bow.

We went out, where Earp and I drew in great lungfuls of fresh air. Holmes chuckled, without mirth.

"My good luck piece benefits me yet again. I took it from a German ironmonger who thought to ingratiate himself with Chancellor Bismarck by flooding the British market and devaluing its currency. Our educated friend inside is neither a liar nor a myopic. His price would exceed Littlejohn's ability to pay, and it's a very good counterfeit."

"Then we're licked," Earp said. "I met Woods. He's short as a rooster and fat as a hog, just like Doc said. No one would confuse them with the moon out."

"I should like to see the scene of the atrocity."

We followed Earp to an open area a hundred yards from the nearest structure, barren but for rocks and scrub and grading downwards from the mining camp, our guide reminding us to be alert for rattlesnakes. The dry earth was scored and spotted with wagon tracks and complex patterns made by overlapping hoof prints.

"A train of supplies and provisions came in from Tucson that night," Earp said. "Littlejohn and Dundy came out to visit, and the teamsters sat around passing the jug. They say Doc came to the top of that rise, coughing and cussing and calling for Littlejohn to show himself. When Littlejohn got up from the ground, Doc plugged him in the belly. That's the story they told, anyway, to the last man."

"Where was Littlejohn standing when he was shot?"

"Right where I am."

"Doctor, will you stand where Mr. Earp indicated that Doc Holliday stood?"

I went to that spot.

"Mr. Earp, could you mistake Dr. Watson for Holliday under these circumstances?"

"No, sir. A bat wouldn't. Watson's a head shorter and twice as thick through the chest."

"What about at night? Disregard for the moment his mode of dress."

"The moon was just shy of full that night. What clothes he had on don't feature. You can make a skinny man look fat in the right clothes, pillows and such, but you can't make a fat man skinny, nor a short man tall, without a pair of stilts."

"I think it's time we met Mr. Woods."

A crude wooden placard hung suspended by twine above the open flap of a tent with wooden framework, reading *Tailor's Shop & Undertaking Parlor, A. Woods, Prop.*, in whitewash. We ducked inside and were greeted by a man who rose from a canvas chair. The fellow was neatly dressed in a striped waistcoat, black garters, and grey flannel trousers, but the first thing one noticed was his unnaturally brief stature—four feet two at the outside—and cherubic roundness. He was highly coloured and close-shaven, with clear blue eyes, and were I his physician I might have treated him for obesity, but never consumption. His welcoming expression became a frown when he recognised Earp.

"Mr. Algernon Woods? I am Sherlock Holmes. This is Dr. Watson, my associate, and I believe you know this other gentleman."

"We met." His voice, astonishingly deep for the size of its chamber, had a harsh edge. "He accused me of hiring someone who looked like Holliday to kill Littlejohn."

"I considered and rejected that hypothesis in the case of Jasper Riley. Youngblood is small and lightly populated as yet. Any local resident who resembled Holliday would be certain to fall under suspicion, and no stranger could fail to be noticed and questioned. In the absence of other suspects, I must conclude that one of three men is a murderer."

"Your man's in jail."

"I understand Holliday made use of your tailoring services."

"He's particular. Grey coats, never black, and he likes his shirts coloured. I doubled the size of my scrap pile with the stuff he rejected." He indicated a heap of odds and ends of cloth between trestle tables covered with bolts of material.

"A man of distinction," Holmes said.

"A man that likes to stand out."

"In his condition he can hardly hope not to. As undertaker, did you conduct a post-mortem examination upon Littlejohn?"

"I dug for the slug, but it passed on through."

"Hardly exhaustive. Has he been interred?"

"Buried? Not yet; he's in back. What are you, Pinkerton?"

"I am merely a visitor with a passion for justice. Would you object if Dr. Watson examined the corpse?"

Woods began to speak, but at that moment Wyatt Earp spread his coat casually, exposing the handle of his revolver. The small man closed his mouth and led us with a waddling gait round the edge of a canvas flap bisecting the tent.

I won't belabour the reader with the clinical details of my examination. At Holmes's direction I probed the ghastly wound, then covered the naked body with a sheet and wiped my hands.

"Downwards trajectory through the abdomen," I said. "Thirty degrees."

"Holliday was taller than Littlejohn," Woods said. "It's natural he would fire at a downward angle."

Holmes didn't appear to be listening. "Mr. Earp, would you say the ground sloped thirty degrees at the scene of the crime?"

"About that. I worked on a track gang once and learned a thing or two about grades."

"Thank you. My compliments, Mr. Woods, upon your reconstructive skills. With rouge and wax you've managed to make Mr. Littlejohn appear in excellent health. Would you allow me to buy you a whisky at the Mescalero Saloon, to apolgise for having wrongly suspected you?"

"I won't drink with Holliday's friend. I don't trust him."

Holmes took Earp aside. The pair spoke in low tones. At length the frontiersman left, but not before casting a dark glance back at Woods over his shoulder.

"Mr. Earp understands and has recused himself from our celebration," Holmes said.

One whisky became three, then four. I am not a man of temperance, but neither am I bibulous, and I measured carefully my ingestion whilst marvelling at the little man's capacity and Holmes's. Their speech grew loud, their consonants less crisp. I had not seen my companion in a state of inebriation and felt embarrassed for him and for my country.

I became distinctly ill at ease as darkness fell and the saloon filled with teamsters and miners, all of whom seemed to share my tablemates' fondness for spirits. I remembered what Holliday had said about a bright moon being ideal for a hanging. Although I had not yet come round to Holmes's point of view regarding the prisoner's innocence, I believed no man should be denied his day in court. The guard at the jail could not withstand a drunken mob, and Earp and I would not greatly alter the odds with my friend in an intoxicated state.

Holmes was insensitive to the danger. He suggested we escort Woods back to his establishment, but in truth, when he rose he was as unsteady on his feet as our guest. I kept my hand in my revolver pocket as we walked through that den of smoke and evil intentions, feeling very much upon my own.

My fears for my companion's clouded faculties were realised when he steered Woods in a direction opposite the path to his tent.

"Holmes," I said, "this isn't—"

He cut me off with a sloppy hiss, a finger to his lips and his other hand clutching the little man's collar, essentially holding him up; Woods was nearly comatose.

Holmes winked at me then. In that moment I knew that he was sober.

Confused and only partially encouraged—for three just men against an enraged herd is scarcely better than two—I accompanied the pair outside the mining camp and down the slope where the murder of Hank Littlejohn had occurred.

"Holmes!" I jerked out my revolver.

A group of men stood at the base of the descent. I recognised Elmer Dundy, Littlejohn's truculent teamster partner, and the miners who had been with him when he'd accosted us in the saloon.

Holmes grasped my wrist. "Spare them, Doctor. They're witnesses."

"Let's get this done with." Dundy's tone now was free of bluster. I considered him more dangerous in this humour than ever. "I came prepared." He held up a length of rope ending in a noose.

"One moment. Mr. Earp?"

"Here."

That fellow strode out of the shadow of a piñon tree into the light of a moon that was, in Holliday's words, "as big as a pumpkin." His revolver was in his hand.

Dundy and his friends fell into growling murmurs. Algernon Woods, who until this moment had been talking and singing to himself, grew silent, and to a great measure less incoherent. "What's this about? Where's my tent?"

"It's Holliday! He's busted out!" One of the miners pointed.

We turned to observe a tall, emaciated figure at the top of the slope, wearing a voluminous pale coat and a broad-brimmed hat that shadowed the top half of his face and the hollows in his cheeks. One bony wrist stuck far out of its sleeve as the figure raised his arm to shoulder level and pointed a long-barrelled revolver directly at Holmes and Woods.

Several of Dundy's friends clawed at their overalls, only to stop at a harsh command from Earp, accompanied by the crackling of the hammer as he levelled his weapon at the crowd.

Holmes, with a foolhardiness I could attribute only to the bottle, left Woods weaving to ascend the slope, straight towards the gunman. When he stood beside the figure at the top, he said, "Observe his stance. Is it habitual with Holliday?"

"Ask anyone," Earp said. "Only fools in dime novels fire from the hip."

"Mr. Dundy?"

The teamster conferred with his friends, nodded. He was hesitant, and with good reason: All could see that Holmes stood two heads higher than the man identified as Holliday.

Holmes produced a ball of string, one end of which he tied to the barrel of the gunman's pistol, then relieved him of it and assumed the former's stance. "Watson!"

I abandoned my weapon to its pocket, the better to catch the spool as he threw it in my direction.

"Mr. Earp, you are Littlejohn's height, are you not?"

"Give or take an inch, I reckon. I only saw him horizontal."

"Kindly take Mr. Woods's place."

But there was nothing kind in the way Earp shoved the little tailor aside and supplanted him. He stood, holding his aim upon the group of witnesses as, seeing Holmes's purpose, I unwound the spool.

"Taut, dear fellow! A bullet observes no principle other than the shortest distance between two points."

I pulled the string tight and placed the spool against Earp's person. It touched him high on the chest.

"Littlejohn was struck low in the abdomen. You will observe, gentlemen, that I stand at about Holliday's height."

No objections were raised. Holmes then returned the pistol to the much shorter man at his side, who raised it to shoulder level and aimed it down the slope. When at this angle I tightened the string, it touched Earp at his abdomen.

"Perspective, gentlemen. A short man standing at an angle thirty degrees higher than the man he is facing must appear taller; but the laws of physics are inviolate." So saying, he snatched the hat off the man dressed as Holliday.

"So sorry." The Chinese opium seller smiled and bowed to his audience. "One pipee apiece, courtesy of Mr. Holmes."

"The thing was simplicity itself," said Holmes, once we were settled in Mrs. Blake's boardinghouse, across from the room where Doc Holliday snored and coughed by turns, resting from his incarceration; or more precisely, from his celebration of same at the Mescalero Saloon. "Woods knew Holliday's sartorial preferences and designed a similar wardrobe for himself whose cuffs fell short of his wrists and whose trousers swung free of his insteps; he was foolish enough to leave it among his scraps, where Earp found it whilst the rest of us sampled the fare at the Mescalero. Had he been unsuccessful, he was to interrupt our drinking session and whisper in my ear. The fact that he did not satisfied me that I had surmised correctly, and I proceeded as we had discussed.

"The subliminal impression created by the costume is of a man too tall for his garb, hence tall. A loose coat implies emaciation regardless of the portliness contained, and an undertaker's knowledge of cosmetics paints hollows in plump cheeks as easily as it fills in the ravages that scoop out flesh in the final stages of debilitating illness. Stir in a pale moon and the shadows cast by a hat with a broad brim, and you have the recipe for a clever sham.

"I am guilty, through Earp, of burgling Woods's store. I also took the liberty of palming a spool of his string during our visit. Coughing and cursing, in Holliday's distinctive Georgia drawl, could only have contributed to the illusion," he continued. "As Woods said himself, Holliday is a man who likes to stand out. The rest was theatre."

I said, "I'll wager it cost you another sovereign to enlist the Chinese's cooperation."

"I rather think he enjoyed performing, and would have done it for half. But what price a man's life, be it even so tenuous and sinister as Holliday's?"

"And what of Woods? That tiny cell won't hold off Dundy's vengeance for long."

"Wyatt Earp has pledged to protect him until the circuit judge arrives. I do believe his passion for justice is equal to mine; as his loyalty to his friend is to yours."

This warmed me more than I could say. I felt that a barrier between us had fallen.

"And what is your gain," I said, "beyond justice?"

He rubbed his hands.

"The chance to drub Wyatt Earp at the game of Faro. I take my profits as they come."

THE ADVENTURE OF THE GREATEST GIFT

"You know, Watson," remarked Sherlock Holmes, "that I am not a religious man. Neither, however, am I a blasphemous one, and I trust I won't offend one of your fine sentiments when I wish that the Great Miracle could be repeated in the case of the late lamented Professor Moriarty. I do miss him these foul evenings."

The date of this pronouncement, according to the notes I have before me, was the twenty-third of December, 1901. The fog that night was particularly dense and yellow, and to peer out through the windows in Holmes's little sitting-room in the quarters we used to share was an exercise in futility: as well gaze into a filthy mirror.

Beneath that Stygian mass of coal-exhaust and vapour, the fresh snowfall of the morning, which had carried such promise of an immaculate Yuletide, had turned as brown as the Thames and clung to hoof and boot alike in sodden clumps. It seemed as if the Great Grimpen Mire of evil memory had spread beyond Devonshire to fill the streets of London. The heavens themselves, it appeared, had joined us in mourning the loss of our good queen, dead these eleven months.

I was concerned by my friend's remark; not because it stung my faith, but for the evidence it gave of the depth of his depression. Weeks had passed since he had last been engaged upon one of the thorny problems that challenged his intellect and distracted him from the unsavoury pursuits that endangered his health. He was never wholly immune to their sinister charms, no matter how long he stayed away from them. Indeed, although the ugly brown bottle and well-worn morocco case containing his needle had gone sufficiently untouched for an industrious spider to have erected a web between them and the corner of the mantelpiece, that gossamer strand posed no barrier to inactivity and *ennui*, which were the only things on the earth that Holmes feared. He dreaded them no more than I did their artificial remedy.

"I should think there are dark enough hearts abroad in a city this size without resuscitating Moriarty," said I, "even in the present season."

I hoped by this to begin a debate that might stimulate him until such time as his thoughts turned in a more wholesome direction. However, his humour remained unchanged.

"Dark enough, perhaps. But black is an exceedingly dull colour without the scarlet stain of imagination. Even the agony columns have nothing more original to offer than the common run of spouse beatings, lost luggage, and straying children. It's enough to make one cancel all his subscriptions." He waved a slim white hand towards the mountainous rubble of crumpled newspapers that had accumulated round the chair in which he sat coiled like Dr. Roylott's adder.

"I imagine those complaints are original enough to the people concerned. Really, Holmes, at times you can be most solipsistic."

He shrugged his shoulders in response, scooped up his charred brier, and filled it with shag from its receptacle of the moment: a plaster cast of the skull of the murderer Burke, the original of which was currently on display at Scotland Yard. The crown of the facsimile had been hinged to tip back for convenient storage.

I plunged ahead. "You once ventured the opinion that your absence from London for any length of time encouraged boldness in the criminal classes. Perhaps you should consider a trip to Paris."

He smiled without mirth. "Good old Watson. You were less transparent when you urged me as my physician to go on holiday, without resorting to subterfuge. I should be just as bored there as here, with the added exasperation of all those cream sauces. No, I shall stay here and await the diversion of a good poisoning."

I should have argued the point further had not someone chosen that moment to ring at the street door.

"Hark!" exclaimed Holmes, shaking out the match with which he had been about to light his pipe. "There is a merry bell, and there to answer it the sturdy tread of our esteemed Mrs. Hudson. She may bring us glad tidings yet."

I heartily joined with him in this hopeful anticipation.

Within moments, his prediction was confirmed. I swung open the door in answer to the landlady's gentle tap and beheld in her hands a curious-looking parcel, a cylinder wrapped in ordinary brown paper and bound with string.

"A delivery for Mr. Holmes, Doctor," said she. "I gave the fellow tuppence."

I handed her that sum and accepted the parcel. It was so light it might have been empty.

"Who delivered it, pray?" asked Holmes, who had unwound himself from his chair with panther quickness at the first touch of her knuckles against the door. He stood behind me crackling with energy, the indolent lounger vanished.

"A commissionaire, sir. He said the package was waiting for him when he reported for duty and no one seems to know who left it."

"Did you believe him?"

That good Scotswoman drew herself up to her not inconsiderable height. "I'd sooner question the character of the prime minister than a veteran."

"The king himself could not have said it better," Holmes said, when we were alone once again. "What do you make of it, old fellow?"

"I should say it's a package of some sort."

"Pawky elf!" He snatched it from my hands and carried it over to the gas lamp, where he studied the object thoroughly from end to end and all round. It was less than five inches in length, with a diameter of some two and one-half inches, and as I said weighed rather less than a common box of matches.

"No return address or postmark, just 'Sherlock Holmes, Esq.' And the address, written in block." He sniffed it. "Petroleum-based ink, obtainable in any stationery shop for less than a shilling. One might wish that obfuscation involved more trouble and expense; but if that is the only conundrum it presents, it's preferable to sitting round pining for a new Napoleon of Crime." He shook it. It made no noise.

"Careful, Holmes! It may be an explosive device."

"If so, it cannot contain enough powder to snuff out a candle. I've examined quite thoroughly the heft and volume of the various volatile compounds in my monograph on demolitions." Absorbed in his contemplation of the bundle, he fished a hand inside his pocket, appeared to realise tardily that he was wearing his dressing-gown, and charged to the deal table where he kept his chemical apparatus and instruments. He used a surgeon's scalpel to cut the string.

The gaily decorated cardboard canister that emerged from the wrapping brought an expression of chagrin to his face that nearly made me smile. Events of a far more startling nature seldom caused him such consternation. The red-and-gold lettering described an undulating pattern across the adhesive label, spelling out 'Edison Gold Moulded Records'.

"It's nothing but a wax recording cylinder!" I cried.

"Your grasp of the obvious is as sound as ever. Its significance is somewhat more obscure."

"Perhaps someone knows you're a lover of music. An anonymous admirer."

"Perhaps." He removed the lid and peered inside. Then he tipped the contents out onto the table. The glistening roll of hardened wax rotated to a stop against the base of his microscope.

"Nothing else inside," Holmes reported, groping at the canister's interior with the ends of his fingers. "The cardboard doesn't appear to have been tampered with. I doubt any messages are hidden between the layers." He set it down and lifted the cylinder, submitting it to the same scrutiny.

"Play it," said I. "It may be a recorded message."

"My conclusion precisely. I shall make a detective of you yet."

He carried the cylinder to the parlour phonograph, a present from the grateful captain of the Pope's Swiss Guard, and slid it into place.

He gave the crank a few turns and applied the needle to the recording. A second or two of hoarse scratching issued from the horn, then the sweet strain of strings, accompanied by the singing of an accomplished male tenor:

> *After the ball is over,*
> *After the break of morn,*
> *After the dancers' leaving,*
> *After the stars are gone.*
> *Many a heart is aching,*
> *If you could read them all;*
> *Many the hopes that have vanished,*
> *After the ball.*

The refrain was repeated, after which the recording scratched into silence. I could make nothing of it, other than that someone had gone to some length to play a joke on the famous detective; but Holmes was galvanised. He charged towards his chair, and there on his knees sorted feverishly through the wrecked newspapers, snapping open the sections and raking them with his eyes, disposing of each as it disappointed him and seizing upon the next. At length he shot to his feet, folding one over.

"Hullo, Watson! Listen to this."

He read:

> *All of London society is expected to gather at*
> *Balderwood House, home of Sir John Whitsunday, M.P.,*
> *and his wife, Alice, where on the 23rd a ball will be held*
> *to honour their guest, the Marquis duBlac, of Paris and*
> *Bordeaux, France. The marquis is popular in this*

country, as his efforts on behalf of the French Republic
to cement peaceful relations between his homeland and
England are well known.

"'After the Ball' is a popular song in America," said I. "Friends in Chicago have written me that they're quite weary of hearing it everywhere they go. How can you be certain the recording refers to this event?"

"You must agree that this particular song arriving on the night of this affair is an unlikely coincidence. Use your imagination: 'Many a heart is aching'; 'Many the hopes that have vanished.' What cataclysm might we expect to cause these tragic considerations?"

I frowned. "War?"

"Bravo! The friendship between duBlac and our government is a slim barricade against the centuries-old differences that have plunged England and France time and again into mass bloodshed. Certain foreign powers would have much to gain by eliminating so well-known a French dignitary on British soil."

"Good heavens! Are you suggesting he may be assassinated at that ball?"

"There is no time to discuss the matter. How soon can you be dressed for a gala evening?"

"Ten minutes from here to my house, and twenty minutes to change." I snatched my coat and hat off the peg.

"I shall be there with a hansom in thirty minutes. Do not forget to add a revolver to your ensemble. A well-armed man is dressed for any occasion."

"How are we to get in without an invitation?"

His eyes were bright. "I am Sherlock Holmes. My presence is always welcome among the law-abiding."

Balderwood House had been built under Charles I, upon the
foundations of a monastery burned to the ground during the
Reformation. In those days it had occupied a country plot far from the
bustle of medieval London: The great fire that had destroyed most of the
city under Charles II had been but a glimmer observed from its casement
windows. In the ensuing three centuries, however, the metropolis had
spread to encompass its walls. A twenty-minute hansom ride deposited
us at the gate, which stood open for the convenience of the evening's
guests. Notwithstanding the gay occasion, the dour fog, and beneath
it the stark fact of a nation bereaved, cast over the estate a sombre,
even baleful aspect. The candles burning in the windows created the
impression that we were under the hostile scrutiny of a many-eyed beast
from pagan mythology. Despite the clammy chill of the evening, drops
of perspiration prickled beneath my boiled shirt.

The butler, a cherubic enough fellow, bald of head and pink of
cheek, frowned decorously at Holmes's admission that we had not been
invited, but accepted our cards and asked us to wait in the entryway.
Moments later we were joined among the room's baronial trappings by
a handsome woman in her middle years, attired in a black evening dress
of dutiful mourning and a minimum of jewels, who introduced herself
as Lady Alice Whitsunday, wife of Sir John.

"And which of you is Mr. Holmes?" asked she eagerly, looking
from one of us to the other. "You do us a great honour, along with
embarrassment that we omitted you from the list of our guests."

Holmes accepted this well-bred rebuke with equal grace, removing
his silk hat.

"I am Holmes, dear madam, and by that confession the man who
must apologise for this breach of protocol. This is Dr. Watson, my
friend and confidant. It is my belief that someone intends to do your
party a great deal more mischief than mine."

"My stars! A theft?" Her hand flew to the pearl choker at her neck.

"No, Lady Alice. A murder."

She paled suddenly, and I stepped forwards. However, she was an estimable lady, and instead of swooning tugged at a bell pull. Instantly the butler reappeared.

"Gregory, please fetch Sir John."

The servant bowed and withdrew. Within a short space of time, the doors to what once must have been the Great Hall slid open, emitting music, sounds of merriment, and the lord of the manor, who drew the doors shut behind him and stood looking down at his two unwanted visitors from his astonishing height. He was a full head taller than my friend, but weighed not a copper more; beneath a shock of startling white hair the very bones of his face protruded beneath his bluish pallor like stones in a shallow pool. The black satin mourning-band sewn to the sleeve of his evening coat was not darker than his gaze.

"What is this outrage?" he demanded coldly.

Holmes wasted no time in niceties.

"My name is Sherlock Holmes. It has come to my attention that your guest of honour is in grave danger. He may not leave this house alive."

"The marquis? Indeed. Where did you obtain this information?"

"There is no time, Sir John. Is there a room where we can be alone with the gentleman?"

Parliament has never been known for swift action. I was impressed, therefore, when this esteemed member directed us immediately to a room at the top of the stairs and joined us there within five minutes, accompanied by the French dignitary. The room was Sir John's study, spacious and scholarly, with books on all sides and claret and cigars on a table opposite his desk, an uncommonly fine one of carved mahogany.

"A very great pleasure, Monsieur 'Olmes. Your services to my country are known in every corner of the Republic. The circumstances surrounding the rescue of Marechal Henri Bonaparte from monarchists is still the talk of Paris."

The marquis was a small man as was common to the Gallic race, with a large head adorned by neatly pointed moustaches. A red satin sash described a violent diagonal across his starched shirtfront, with the golden starburst of the *Legion d'Honneur* appended to his right breast. He bowed deeply.

"I hope to do it one more service this night, on behalf of both our homelands, your excellency," replied Holmes.

He proceeded to tell both duBlac and our host, in the sparest possible terms, the circumstances that had led us to this meeting.

"What rot!" said Sir John, when he'd finished. "You propose to disrupt an important affair of state on the basis of a trinket you received in the post?"

"Disruption is not my intent, and we should all be wise to pay particular attention to trinkets. The fates of kingdoms often turn upon such trifles."

"I agree with Monsieur 'Olmes," said the Frenchman. "A necklace led to the fall of the Bastille and the Reign of Terror. What do you propose to do?" he asked Holmes.

"Nothing, your excellency."

"Nothing?" The honoured guest's great brow creased.

"Nothing!" Patches of unhealthy colour appeared upon Sir John's hollow cheeks.

"Holmes!" Even I, who knew never to expect anything but the unexpected where my companion's methods were concerned, was astounded.

"Then I trust you will have no objection to my sending Gregory out for the police." Sir John reached for a bell pull beside the desk.

Holmes held up an admonitory hand.

"Forgive me for assuming too much, Sir John. There is no reason to expect a busy M.P. to be familiar with the lyrics to a popular American song. I call your attention to the first stanza."

Whereupon the greatest detective in England astonished us all further by singing, in a pleasant tenor:

After the ball is over,
After the break of morn,
After the dancers' leaving—

"The message is clear," he said, abandoning the rest of the composition. "Our assassin will not strike before the end of the evening. If we disrupt the entertainment with an aggressive investigation, we will put him on alert, and merely postpone the inevitable until another time when we are less prepared. Whoever our unknown benefactor is—we shall assume for now he is a traitor in the enemy camp—we must not waste the clue he has sent us by behaving rashly."

Our reluctant host withdrew his hand from the bell pull. "Do you mean to suggest that we go on with the ball as if we knew nothing?"

"That is the impression we must leave, and it is not far from the truth. In reality, of course, we shall be wary. Is there a location from where Dr. Watson and I can observe the activity in the ballroom without calling attention to ourselves?"

"There is a landing on this floor where you can stand between the staircases and look down. There will likely be other guests there," added Sir John with a faint hint of apology. The gravity displayed by his illustrious intruder had to some degree eroded his disbelief.

"All the better for us to lose ourselves in the crowd. *Au revoir*, your excellency." Holmes executed a smart bow in the marquis' direction.

"I pray that you will be able to enjoy your fete without fear for your safety."

"I do not see how it could be otherwise, with the great Sherlock Holmes as my protector. In any event, once you have faced Prussian cannon, you find that life is"—he hesitated—"*surprix*, what is the English word?"

"Overpriced. *Vous somme un chevalier, excellence.*"

The Frenchman took his leave. Following, Sir John Whitsunday interrupted his own departure to peer down at my friend. "I should warn you that if it turns out my guest's trust is misplaced, you will have to answer to all of Europe."

"Thank you. I am not so concerned at that as I am of answering to myself."

The ballroom had been refurbished in the grand Victorian manner, with a high vaulted ceiling and twin staircases swooping down from a balustrated landing. As we climbed the steps, having left our sticks and outerwear in the study, I said, "Holmes, I've known you for twenty years and never heard you speak more than a common phrase in French before tonight."

"I picked it up during the Bonaparte affair the marquis mentioned—a simple matter, not a worthy subject for your memoirs. Learning required little effort, beyond inserting a string of unnecessary letters into one-syllable words."

At the top we stood among a group of gentlemen elders who had sought refuge from the energetic activity on the floor to smoke cigars and pontificate upon the situation in Ireland. To one who recalled the bright hues and laughter of happier times, it was somewhat depressing to observe the subdued fashions of the dancers moving decorously to restrained music from an orchestra clad in black from neck to heels. Even the wreaths and coloured glass ornaments that decorated the hall were understated to a funereal degree.

Holmes, I saw, was in no such reverie. In spite of his own assurance that nothing would happen for several hours, his hatchetlike profile and intense gaze as he gripped the marble railing made him resemble a bird of prey. I slid my hand into my coat pocket and found comfort in the cool touch of my old service revolver, veteran of so many adventures.

I directed my attention to the marquis, who stood drinking wine and chatting with the Whitsundays beneath a huge full-length portrait of our late queen, suitably framed in black crepe. When that proved uninvolving, for some time I endeavoured to pick out the villain or villains who had infiltrated the gathering. It seemed that this swarthy fellow standing by the refreshments table fit the bill, but then that nervous dancer drew my suspicions regarding the source of his unease.

Such diversions are contagious; at the end of an hour I had decided that everyone present, with the exceptions of my friend and I, our hosts, and of course the marquis himself, was capable of assassination. Holmes had told me time and time again that I lacked imagination, but at that juncture I decided I had it in surplus.

Then a stout, red-faced guest who shared our landing raised his voice in argument with a companion, loudly excoriating the French government for criticising our stand against the Boers. He could be overheard above the music, and as far as the ballroom floor, where annoyed glances rose his way. The vehemence of his tirade caused me to share my suspicions with Holmes in a hoarse whisper.

"That is Colonel Sutworth," said he. "He's been in the House of Commons since Gladstone was a lad. In any case, I have eliminated all the men on this landing, so long as they remain upon it. Their tailoring will not admit the accessory of an air rifle or a crossbow. The range is too great for any accuracy with a revolver."

"Have you eliminated the women present tonight?"

"Nothing would please me more. Daggers and poison are their weapons of choice, and I do not relish wrestling one to the floor the moment she moves within striking distance of duBlac or his wine."

"Perhaps we should move closer. 'After the break of morn' may be a ruse to divert us from the actual timetable."

"I considered that, and rejected it immediately. If subterfuge were intended, why alert us at all? In any case, I would postulate a later hour even without the lyric. The floor is too crowded for the killer to make good his escape. He will wait until the guests thin out."

I resolved thenceforth to withhold my opinions, which were clearly an irritation to my companion.

Sometime later I suppressed a yawn and withdrew my hand from my weapon to reach for my watch. Holmes's sudden grip upon my arm arrested the movement. Belatedly I became aware of the tune the orchestra was playing:

After the ball is over . . .

He cursed beneath his breath. "I've been a fool, Watson! The clue was not in the lyrics, but in the song itself. It is a signal for action!"

"But the killer's escape—"

"No time to explain!"

With that, he was gone from my side, flying down the stairs with his coattails flying.

I sprinted to catch up, drawing my revolver and shouldering aside a number of guests who were climbing the steps to escape the heat and noise of the ballroom. Several well-dressed gentlemen complained of the effrontery in no uncertain terms. A middle-aged woman in black taffeta shrieked when she spied my weapon.

By the time I quit the stairs, Holmes was halfway across the floor, shoving men and women sprawling in his anxiety to reach the guest of honour. I hastened behind, dodging and leaping over the hunched forms of outraged dancers attempting to regain their feet. I overheard a Scotsman declare in an angry, burring baritone that this was what one might expect now that Edward was on the throne.

Now the refreshments table was the only thing separating Sherlock Holmes from the emperilled marquis. He seized the table in both hands and flung it over. It was a twelve-foot trestle, and it went down in a flurry of white linen, flashing silver, and shattering crystal as Holmes vaulted on over, bound for the shocked trio of duBlac, Sir John, and Lady Alice.

I am not as athletic as my friend; years of overindulgence have thickened my girth and shortened my endurance. I paused before the ruined table, panting heavily; and was immediately grateful that I had, for as I glanced up, I experienced a hallucination so real, the shock might have flung me on my face in mid-stride.

Queen Victoria was moving.

Moving, I repeat, with the same stately dignity with which she had comported herself in life, advancing in my direction while the crowd on the dance floor parted to make her a path.

Presently I realised that this was a misapprehension, and that the great seven-foot portrait that hung behind the marquis and his hosts was swinging outward, as on a pivot. Beyond it yawned the dark rectangular of an open passage, and inside that rectangle, standing poised within easy striking distance of the French dignitary with a long-bladed dagger was—

But I am drawing ahead of my narrative. In that frenzied moment, I saw only the great blubbery figure of a man in immaculate evening dress, his flipper of a right hand engulfing his weapon to the hilt.

I drew aim upon that broad target with my revolver, but Holmes himself prevented me from squeezing the trigger, for as he leapt to fling his arms round the man in the passage, his back came between us. I held my fire whilst the pair fell into a heap on the floor inside the opening.

"Hold, Sherlock!" the huge man exclaimed, disentangling himself from the detective. "Whenever will you learn to place your head before your feet?"

It was then that I recognised Mycroft Holmes, my friend's older brother, from whose hand the dagger had fallen when he crashed to earth.

Ten minutes later, Holmes and I were seated in our host's commodious study with Sir John, the Marquis duBlac, and Mycroft, who had corrected his dishevelment and now occupied the largest armchair with a cigar in hand and a glass of claret on the table at his elbow.

"All your questions will be answered in the fullness of time," said he. "Impatience always was your great weakness, Sherlock. A man with less natural protection than I might have suffered a cracked rib."

"As might I," responded his brother, "had I not an enormous feather mattress to break my fall." The sharpness of this retort gave evidence of the mixture of curiosity and resentment that roiled beneath Holmes's otherwise calm exterior.

Mycroft ignored the aspersion. "As the elder brother, I shall go first. Tell us how you guessed at the presence of a secret passage behind the painting."

"I haven't guessed since we were children. When the orchestra began playing 'After the Ball' and I realised the die was cast, a hidden corridor was the only possibility that occurred to me. It offered both access to the intended victim and escape afterwards. The antiquity of Balderwood House suggested the probability that such a feature existed. Fairer circumstances did not prevent the Catholic clergy from designing priest-holes for concealment in the event of further persecution."

"Admirable!" cried the marquis. "Unfortunately, our society includes a number of deranged individuals for whom the prospect of flight holds no importance."

"There is no allowing for the movements of such men—or women, if your Charlotte Corday is any example. However, the wax recording cylinder that was delivered to my door, and the whole business of the song, pointed to a subtle and devious mind. A fanatic did not answer."

"Close plotters have been known to employ fanatics," Mycroft reminded him.

His brother shook his head. "The prize was too great, and as I said, the deranged are unpredictable, a danger to their masters as well as to their opponents. Skilled labour demands a steady hand."

Sir John sat back and crossed his long legs, exhibiting calm for the first time. I began to see then that his apoplectic display had been just that: a show to throw us off the trail.

"He is brilliant, as well as cool under fire. Gentlemen, I withdraw all my objections. I feared that Holmes was an invention of fiction, but his performance tonight convinces me he is the man for us."

"I was never in doubt." The Frenchman's eyes twinkled. "Dr. Watson's accounts of his friend's adventures are very popular in my country. The Marechal Bonaparte business confirmed their veracity, but I was not present on that occasion. I am now privileged to have witnessed his genius and daring at firsthand."

"I felt sure you would see it my way, your excellency," put in Mycroft. "I was not so certain of Sir John, and so remained neutral."

Here, Holmes demonstrated the impatience that his brother deplored. His eyes were as bright and sharp as Mycroft's dagger, and there were patches of high colour on his cheeks.

"The time has come to tell me the purpose of this charade. You haven't the ambition, brother, for practical jokes, which in any case would be unseemly in the shadow of our recent loss."

Mycroft pulled at his cigar. "That loss has led to a most unstable situation upon the continent. For some time now, the great powers have known that certain devious men hope to turn the change of leadership into unrest, and seize large parts of British and French territories by arranging a war between our two countries that would weaken us both. It does not stress the imagination to predict that a global conflict would result. However, we could not come to an agreement as to who should be entrusted with investigating and uncovering the details of their plans. Until now." He drew a folded sheet of paper from inside his coat and handed it to his brother.

Holmes spread the exquisite stationery, examined both sides, and read. The text was all but obscured by the presence of royal seals.

"What is the purpose of this?" he asked at length.

Mycroft said, "It is a letter signed and sealed by all the crowned heads of Europe and Great Britain, presenting the bearer with authority to go anywhere and interrogate anyone, with the absolute cooperation of the local constabulary. Your mission will be to investigate any and all rumours of subversive activity and to report your conclusions to an international tribunal headquartered in Switzerland. You will answer to no government; which means, of course, that you will answer to them all."

At this point, the broad face of this shadowy influence in British politics became stern.

"Before you accept this post," said he, "I should warn you that it will expose you to more danger than you have known previously. In addition, it will leave you little time for quiet contemplation. I can promise you it will never be boring."

"I begin to understand," said Holmes. "Tonight was an audition."

His brother's scowl became a sardonic smile.

"I must claim credit for the sham's details. I'm inordinately proud of the business with the wax cylinder. It arrived by the international post with others, a musical library; an early Christmas present from an American dignitary, which I decided to put to good use. I was somewhat concerned when Sir John reported that you did not expect anything to happen until the ball was concluded—really, Sherlock, you must learn to curb your impulses before you enter the Great Game—but I must compliment you upon the swiftness of your actions the moment you realised you'd erred. Flexibility and reflex are crucial. Do you accept the post?"

"I can do no other in the name of peace. I'm grateful you chose me."

"You should thank Dr. Watson."

"Watson? Whatever for?"

"He visited me last week in my offices in Whitehall, reminded me sternly that England was wasting its greatest natural resource and challenging me to put you to work on its behalf. I confess that because I am related to you I lacked the objectivity to have considered you for this assignment. It was good luck all round that he approached me when he did."

Holmes looked at me with the first signs of absolute astonishment I had ever seen upon his face. I hastened to reassure him—if reassurance were necessary—that he had not lost his keen powers of observation.

"I knew nothing of this test, Holmes. Mycroft said only that he would take up my suggestion with the foreign secretary. He seemed distracted, and I assumed that he was merely humouring me so that he could return to work. I'd nearly forgotten our meeting, and was convinced tonight's mystery was legitimate."

"Thank you for that, old fellow, but you might have spared your breath. I know you well enough to know you are incapable of guile."

I could not think how to respond to this rather sinister compliment, and so kept silent.

"A great adventure!" the marquis exclaimed.

"It is more than that." Holmes was still looking at me. "It is a great gift from a great friend."

At that moment the clock on Sir John Whitsunday's mantelpiece chimed midnight, announcing that Christmas Eve was upon us.

"The ball is over, Watson. Let us not overstay our welcome."

"Happy Christmas, Holmes," said I.

My friend made no reply. His store of sentiment was exhausted. It was never ample.

My doorbell rang on Christmas morning while I was breakfasting with my wife.

"Oh, dear." She set down her cup. "I hope that isn't a patient, today of all days."

I arose from the table resignedly. "Perhaps it is just Mrs. Ablewhite's annual case of the sniffles. Asafetida, and her son can handle the mustard-plaster after I leave."

A fat commissionaire stood upon the doorstep, his great bulging middle barely contained by his brass buttons. An enormous pair of snow-white moustaches obscured most of his florid face. "Package for Dr. Watson," said he.

I signed the receipt and accepted the parcel, which was no larger than a tin of tobacco and wrapped in bright silver paper. Curious to see which of my patients had sent me a gift, I unwrapped it there upon the threshold.

It was a box containing Sherlock Holmes's needle in its morocco leather case and his bottle of cocaine.

"Happy Christmas, Watson," came a familiar voice from behind the messenger's moustaches. "Thanks to you, I shan't be needing it again this century."

THE DEVIL
AND SHERLOCK
HOLMES

he year 1899 stands out of particular note in my memory; not because it was the last but one of the old century (the numerologists are clear upon this point, but popular opinion differs), but because it was the only time during my long and stimulating association with Sherlock Holmes that I came to call upon his unique services as a client.

It was the last day of April, and because I had not yet made up my mind whether to invest in South African securities, I was refreshing my recollection by way of recent numbers of the *Times* and *Telegraph* about developments in the souring relationship between the Boers and the British in Johannesburg. The day was Sunday, and my professional consulting-room was empty. This situation presented the happy prospect of uninterrupted study outside the melancholy surroundings of my lonely quarters in my wife's temporary absence, as well as a haven from personal troubles of more recent vintage.

I was, therefore, somewhat disgruntled to be forced to disinter myself from the pile of discarded sections to answer the bell.

"Ah, Watson," greeted Sherlock Holmes. "When I find you squandering your day of rest in conference with your cheque-book, I wonder that I should have come in chains, to haunt you out of your miser's destiny."

I was always pleased to encounter my oldest of friends, and wrung his hand before I realised that he had once again trespassed upon my private reflections. It was not until I had relieved him of his hat, ulster, and stick, and we were comfortable in my worn chairs with glasses of brandy in hand to ward off the spring chill, that I asked him by what sorcery he'd divined my late activity.

"The printers' ink upon your hands, on a day when no newspapers are delivered, is evidence; the rest is surmise, based upon familiarity with the company and the one story that has claimed the interest of every journal in the country this past week. Having experienced war at firsthand, you are scarcely an enthusiast of sword-rattling rhetoric; but you are a chronic investor, who prides himself upon his determination to wrest every scrap of intelligence from a venture before he takes the plunge. The rest is simple arithmetic."

"You haven't lost your touch," said I, shaking my head.

"And yet I fear I shall, should I remain in this calm another week. There isn't a criminal with imagination left on our island. They have all emigrated to America to run for public office."

His voice was jocular, but he appeared drawn. I recognised with alarum the look of desperation which had driven him to unhealthy practices in the past. Instead, he had come to me, and I was heartily glad to serve as substitute.

"Well, I don't propose to ask you to investigate the *Uitlanders* in South Africa," I remarked.

He threw his cigarette, which he had just lit, into the grate, a gesture of irritation.

"The fare would be a waste. Anyone with eyes in his head can see there will be war, and that it will be no holiday for Her Majesty's troops. Heed my advice and restrict your gambling to the turf."

Holmes was prickly company when he was agitated. Fortunately, I did not have to cast far to strike a subject that might distract him from his boredom, which in his case could be fatal. The situation had been nearly as much on my mind of late as the squabbling on the Ivory Coast. However, a cautious approach was required, as the circumstances were anathema to his icy faculties of reason.

"As a matter of fact," I teased, "I have been in the way of a matter that may present some features of interest. However, I hesitate to bring it up."

"Old fellow, this is no time in life to acquire discretion. It suits you little." He lifted his head, as a hound does when the wind shifts from the direction of a wood where game is in residence.

"My dear Holmes, let's pretend I said nothing. The thing is beneath you."

"You are an open book, unequal to the skills of a confidence-man dangling bait. Get on with you, and leave the techniques of obverse alienism to the likes of Dr. Freud." In spite of the irony in his speech, he was well and truly on the scent.

"It is just that I know your opinions on the subject."

"What subject is that?" he demanded.

"The supernatural."

"Bah! Spare me your bogey tales."

He pretended disappointment, but I knew him better than to accept appearances. He could disguise his person from me with wigs and rubber noses, but not his smouldering curiosity.

"You are aware, perhaps, that I am a consulting physician to the staff of St. Porphyry's Hospital in Battersea?"

"I know St. Poor's," he said. "My testimony at the Assizes sent a murderer there, bypassing the scaffold, and there are at least two bank robbers jittering in front of gullible medical experts who ought to be rotting in Reading Gaol."

I could not determine whether he was wishing incarceration upon the robbers or the doctors. Either way, I was annoyed.

"St. Porphyry's is a leader in the modern treatment of lunacy. It's not a bolt-hole for charlatans."

"I did not mean to suggest it was. Pray continue. This penchant for withholding the most important feature until the end may please the readers of your tales, but it exhausts my store of patience."

"To be brief," said I, "there is a patient there at present who's convinced himself he's the Devil."

He nodded thoughtfully. "That's on its way towards balancing the account. Bedlam has two Christs and a Moses."

"Have they succeeded in convincing anyone besides themselves?"

He saw my direction, and lit another cigarette with an air of exaggerated insouciance. Thus did I know he was sniffing at the pit I had dug and covered with leaves.

"It's no revelation that he's found some tormented souls in residence who agree with him. There's more sport in bear-baiting."

"It isn't just some of the patients, Holmes," I said, springing the trap. "There are at least two nurses on the staff, and one doctor, who are absolutely unshakeable in the conviction that this fellow is Satan Incarnate."

Within the hour, we were aboard a coach bound for Battersea, the telegraph poles clicking past, quite in time with the working of Holmes's brain. He hammered me with questions, seeking to string the morsels of information I'd already provided into a chronological narrative. It was an old trick of his, not unlike the process of mesmerisation; he worried me for every detail, mundane though it may have been, and in so doing caused me to recall incidents that had been related to me, and which I had seen for myself, but had since forgotten.

My regular practice having stagnated, I had succumbed at last to persistent entreaties from my friend and colleague, Dr. James Menitor, chief alienist at St. Porphyry's, to observe the behaviour of his more challenging patients twice a week and offer my opinion upon their treatment. In this I suspect he thought my close exposure to Holmes's detective techniques would prove useful, and I had been rather too flattered by his determination, and intrigued by the diversion, to put him off any longer.

Dr. Menitor was particularly eager to consult with me in the case of a patient known only as John Smith; at which point in my narration I was interrupted by a derisive snort from Holmes.

"A *nom de romance*," said he, "lacking even the virtue of originality. If I cannot have imagination in my criminals, let me at least have it in my lunatics."

"It was the staff who christened him thus, in lieu of any other identification. Dr. Menitor insists upon treating patients as individuals, not as mere case numbers. Smith was apprehended verbally accosting strollers along the Thames, and committed by Scotland Yard for observation. It seems he told the constable that he was engaged on his annual expedition to snare souls."

"I hadn't realised there was a season. When was this?"

"Three days ago. It was fortuitous you dropped in upon me when you did, for Mr. Smith has indicated he will be returning to the netherworld this very night."

"*Walpurgisnacht*," said Holmes.

"Bless you," said I; for I thought he had sneezed.

"Thank you, but I am quite uncongested. *Walpurgisnacht* is a Teutonic superstition; not worthy of discussion in our scientific age, but possibly of interest to the deluded mind. Has your John Smith a foreign accent?"

"No. As a matter of fact, his speech is British upper class. I wonder that no one has reported him missing."

"I know a number of families in the West End with good reason not to in that situation." He shrugged. "It appears I am guilty, then, of a non sequitur. The date may not be significant. What has he done to support his claim, apart from wandering the hospital corridors, snatching at gnats?"

"Would that were the case. He has already nearly caused the death of one patient and jeopardised the career of a nurse whose professional behaviour was impeccable before he arrived."

Holmes's eyes grew alight in the reflection of the match he had set to his pipe. Violence and disgrace were details dear to his detective's heart.

I continued my report. On his first day in residence, Smith was observed in close whispered conversation with a young man named Tom Turner, who suffered from the conviction that he was Socrates, the ancient Greek sage. Dr. Menitor had been pleased with Turner's progress since he'd been admitted six months previously, wearing a bedsheet wrapped about him in the manner of a toga, bent over and speaking in a voice cracked with age, when in fact he was barely four-and-twenty; he had of his own volition recently resumed contemporary dress, and had even commenced to score off his delusion with self-deprecating wit, an encouraging sign that sanity was returning.

All that changed after his encounter with John Smith.

Minutes after the pair separated, young Turner had opened a supply closet and was prevented from ingesting the contents of a bottle of chlorine bleach only by strenuous intervention by a male orderly who'd happened to be passing. Placed in restraints in the infirmary, the young man raved in his cracked old voice that he must have his hemlock, else how could Socrates fulfill his destiny?

"A madman who reads Plutarch. Perhaps not such an oddity after all."

"Holmes, please!" I deplored his callousness.

"*Mea culpa*, my friend. Pray continue, and I shall endeavour not to be impertinent."

Mollified, I went on.

Confronted by Dr. Menitor after the episode, John Smith smiled blandly.

"Good physician," he said, "when he was Socrates, his acquaintance was worthy of pursuing, but as a plain pudding of the middle class, he was a bore. I am overstocked with Tom Turners, but my inventory of great philosophers is dangerously low."

"Holmes," said I, "neither Menitor nor myself can explain just what Smith said to Turner that overturned the work of months. He will not be drawn out upon the subject."

"And what of the disgraced nurse?"

"Martha Brant has worked at St. Porphyry's for twenty years without so much as a spot on her record. It was her key to the supply closet Turner had in his possession when he was apprehended."

"Stolen?"

"Given, by her own account."

"Hum."

"When questioned, she confessed to removing the key from its ring and surrendering it to Turner. She insisted that she was commanded to do so by Smith. She became hysterical during the interrogation. Dr. Menitor was forced to sedate her with morphine and confine her to a private room, where she remains, attended by another nurse on the staff. Before she lost consciousness, Miss Brant insisted that Smith is the Prince of Lies, precisely as he claims."

"What has been done with Smith in the meantime?"

"At present, he is locked up in the criminal ward. However, that has not stopped him from exercising an unhealthy influence upon all of St. Porphyry's. Since his incarceration, a previously dependable orderly has been sacked for stealing food from the kitchen pantry and selling it to the owner of a public-house in the neighbourhood, and restlessness among the patients has increased to the point where Menitor refuses to step outside his own consulting-room without first placing a loaded revolver in his pocket. The orderlies have all been put on their guard, for an uprising is feared.

"It's for my friend I'm concerned," I continued. "He has been forced to replace the nurse in charge of Miss Brant and assign her to less demanding duties elsewhere in the hospital; the poor girl has come to agree with her that Smith is the Devil. It's true that she's a devout Catholic, belonging to an order that believes in demonic obsession and the cleansing effects of exorcism. However, Miss Brant herself is a down-to-earth sort who was never before heard to express any opinion that was not well-founded in medical science. And when I was there yesterday, I found Menitor in a highly agitated state, and disinclined to rule out the Black Arts as a cause for his present miseries. I fear the situation has unhinged him.

"I hope you will consider me your client in this affair," I concluded.

"Hum," said Holmes again, and pulled at his pipe. "Under ordinary circumstances, I would dismiss this fellow Smith as nothing more than a talented student of the principles taught by the late Franz Mesmer. However, I doubt even that estimable practitioner was capable of entrancing the entire population of a London hospital."

"It is more than that. I've met the fellow, and I can state with absolute certainty that I've never encountered anyone who impressed me so thoroughly that he is the living embodiment of evil. This was before the Turner incident, and we exchanged nothing more than casual greetings; yet his mere presence filled me with dread."

"Insanity is a contagion, Watson. I've seen it before, and no amount of persuasion will force me to concede that prolonged exposure to it is less dangerous than an outbreak of smallpox. Do you limit your visits to St. Poor's, lest you contract it as well. I have never been stimulated by your intellect, but I have come to rely upon your granite pragmatism. Sense is not common, and wisdom is anything but conventional. You must guard them as if they were the crown jewels."

"Is it then your theory that this situation may be explained away as mass hysteria?"

"I refuse to theorise until I have made the acquaintance of Mr. John Smith."

St. Porphyry's Hospital was Georgian, but only in so far as it had been rebuilt from the ruins of the Reformation. Parts of it dated back to William the Conqueror, and I once knew an antiquarian who insisted it was constructed on the site of a Roman temple. It had been by turns a redoubt, a prison, and an abbey, but the addition of some modern architectural features had softened somewhat the medieval gloom I felt whenever I entered its grounds; but not today. The air itself crawled with the horrors of human sacrifice.

The dread sensation increased when we crossed the threshold. An agitated orderly conducted us down the narrow corridor that led past the common room—the heavy door to which was locked up tight—to Dr. Menitor's consulting-room at the back. A stout rubber truncheon hung from a strap round his wrist, and he gripped it with knuckles white. The ancient walls seemed to murmur an unintelligible warning as we passed; it was the sound of the patients, muttering to themselves behind locked doors. This general confinement was by no means a common practice in that establishment. It had been added since my last visit.

We found my friend Menitor in an advanced state of nervous excitement, worse than the one I had left him in not twenty-four hours before. He appeared to have lost weight, and his fallen face was as white as his hair, which I had sworn still bore traces of its original dark colour at our parting. He shook our hands listlessly, dismissed the orderly with an air of distraction, and addressed my companion in a bleating tone I scarcely credited as his.

"I am honoured, Mr. Holmes," said he, "but I fear even your skills are no match for the fate that has befallen this institution to which I have dedicated my entire professional life. St. Porphyry's is damned."

"Has something happened since I left?" I asked, alarumed by his resignation.

"Two of my best orderlies have quit, and I've taken to arming the rest, much good has it done them. None will go near Room Six, even to push a plate of bread through the portal in the door. 'You cannot starve the Devil,' said one, when I attempted to upbraid him for this insubordination. And who am I to lay blame? I'd sooner face a pack of Rider Haggard's lions than approach that colony of Hell."

"Come, come." Holmes was impatient. "Consider: If Smith's assertion is genuine, no door fashioned by the hand of Man can hold him. His continued presence there is proof enough he's either mad or a charlatan."

"You don't know him, Mr. Holmes. We're just his playthings. It pleases him at present to remain where he is and turn brave men into cowards and good women into familiars. When he tires of that, he'll slither out through the bars and bid the maws of the underworld to open and swallow us all."

His voice rose to a shrill cackle—cut off suddenly, as by the sheer will of whatever reason he retained within him.

I went into action without waiting for Holmes's signal. I forced him into a chair with my hand upon his shoulder, strode to the cabinet where he kept a flask of brandy, poured a generous draught into a glass, and commanded him to drink.

He drank off half the elixir in one motion. It seemed to fortify him. He took another sip and set the glass on the corner of his desk. Colour climbed his sallow cheeks.

"Thank you, John. I apologise, Mr. Holmes. I don't mind telling you I've questioned my own rationality throughout this affair. It's more comforting to believe myself mad than to accept the only other explanation that suggests itself."

Holmes's own cold tones were as bracing as the spirits.

"Only the sane question their sanity, Doctor. Until this business is concluded, however, I suggest you let Haggard be and turn your attention towards the Messrs. Gilbert and Sullivan. Their shoguns and pirates are healthier fare in trying times. Later, perhaps, you will agree to collaborate with me on a monograph about the unstable nature of the criminal mind in general. Certainly only an irrational individual would consider committing a felony as long as Sherlock Holmes is in practice."

"Bless you, sir, for the attempt; but I fear I've passed the point where an outrageous remark will lift the bleakness from my soul. Smith has taken the hindmost, and that unfortunate is I."

At that moment, the clock upon his mantel struck seven. Menitor started.

"Five hours left!" he moaned. "He's pledged to quit this world at midnight, and we shall all accompany him."

"I, for one, never embark upon a long voyage without first taking the measure of the captain," Holmes said. "Where is the key to Room Six?"

A great deal of persuasion, and another injection of brandy, were necessary before Dr. Menitor would part with the key to the room in which John Smith had been shut. He wore it, like the poetic albatross, on a cord round his neck. Holmes took it from his hand and instructed me to stay behind with Menitor.

I shook my head. "I'm going with you. We've faced every other devil together. Why not the Dark Lord himself?"

"Your other friend needs you more."

"He will sleep. I slipped a mild solution of morphine into his second drink." In fact, Menitor was already insensate in his chair, with a more peaceful expression upon his face than he had worn in days.

Holmes nodded curtly. "Then by all means, let us deal with the devil we don't know."

The criminal ward occupied most of the ancient keep, with Room Six at the top. Sturdy bars in the windows separated the occupant from a hundred-foot drop to the flags below. I had brought my old service revolver, and Holmes instructed me to stand back with it cocked and in hand as he turned the key in the lock.

This precaution proved unnecessary, as we found the patient seated peacefully upon the cot that represented the room's only furnishing. He was dressed neatly but simply in the patched clothing that had been donated to the hospital by the city's charitable institutions, and the shoes he'd worn when he was brought there, shiny black patent-leathers to match his formal dress, from which all the tailor's labels had been removed.

In appearance, there was little about John Smith to support his demonic claim. He was fair, with a windblown mop of blonde curls, moustaches in need of trimming, and a sprinkling of golden whiskers to attest to his three days without a razor. He was a dozen or so pounds overweight. I should have judged his age to be about thirty, and yet there was a quality in his eyes—large, and of the palest blue imaginable—that suggested the bleakness of an uninhabited room, as if they had witnessed more than one lifetime and remained unchanged.

There was, too, an attitude of mockery in his smile, outwardly polite and welcoming, that seemed to reduce everything and everyone he turned it upon to insignificance. I do not know if it was these features or the man himself who filled me with such dread and loathing. I closed the door and stationed myself with my back to it, the revolver in my pocket now, but still cocked in my hand.

"Mr. Sherlock Holmes," he greeted in his soft, modulated voice, gentled further by a West End accent. "The engravings in the public journals do you little justice. You have the brow of a philosopher."

"Indeed? A late gentleman of my acquaintance once remarked that there was less frontal development than he'd expected."

"Dear Professor Moriarty. Thank you for that unexpected gift. I did not have him down for another decade when you pitched him over those falls."

Holmes was unimpressed by this intelligence; the story of his last meeting with that blackguardly academic was well known to readers of the account I had published in *The Strand* magazine.

"Shall I address you familiarly as Lucifer, or Your Dark Majesty?" Holmes asked evenly. "I'm ignorant as to the protocol."

"Smith will do. I find it difficult to keep track of all my titles myself. How did you make out on that Milverton affair, by the way? The Drey-fuss business had me distracted."

At this Holmes hesitated, and I was hard put to disguise my astonishment. The case of the late blackmailer Charles Augustus Milverton had only recently been concluded, in a most shocking fashion, and its circumstances enjoined me from reporting it publicly for an indefinite period. Holmes's involvement was unknown even to Scotland Yard.

He changed the subject, dissembling his own thoughts on Smith's sources.

"I have come to ask you what was your motive in attempting to destroy Tom Turner," said he. "I shan't accept that fable you told Dr. Menitor."

Smith replied, "I must have my amusements. Arranging wars and corrupting governments requires close concentration over long periods. You have your quaint chemical experiments to divert you from your labours upon your clients' behalf; I have my pursuit of unprepossessing souls. Exquisite miniatures, I call them. One day I hope to show you my display."

"It's a pity Turner escaped your net."

"Fortunately, St. Porphyry's offers a variety of other possibilities." The patient appeared unmoved by Holmes's thrust.

"So I am told. A career ruined, another besmirched, and a third severely straitened. Will you add violent insurrection to your exhibit?"

"Alas, there may not be time. I depart at midnight."

"Do you miss home so much?"

"I am not going home just yet. If Menitor gave you that impression, he misunderstood me. This has been a pleasant holiday, but there is work for me in Whitehall and upon the continent. Your Foreign Secretary shows indications of being entirely too reasonable at Bloemfontein, and the Kaiser is far too comfortable with his country's borders. Also, the Americans have grown complacent with the indestructibility of their presidents. A trip abroad may be warranted. It isn't as if the situation at home will go to Hell in my absence." He chuckled.

"Blighter!" I could no longer restrain myself.

He turned that infernal smile upon me, and with it those vacant, soulless eyes.

"I congratulate you, Doctor. In matters of detective science you remain Holmes's trained baboon, but as a master of classic British understatement you have no peer."

"Your own grasp of the obvious comes close," Holmes observed. "How pedestrian that you should choose this of all nights to plan your escape."

"It's hardly an escape. It's pleased me to have stayed this long in residence. *Walpurgisnacht*, that brief excursion when dead walk and witches convene, has a paralysing effect upon those who still credit it. However, it requires renewal from time to time. Perhaps after tonight, you will believe as well."

Holmes made a little bow. "I accept the challenge, Mr. Smith. We shall return at midnight."

"Shall I offer you kingdoms then?"

The detective paused with his hand on the door. "I beg your pardon?"

"I should admire to have you sit at my right hand throughout eternity, as your mind is nearly as clever and devious as my own. Upon second thought, however, kingdoms would offer you scarce temptation, as any comic-opera monarch who has tried to purchase your loyalty with promises of great wealth can attest. Cocaine, perhaps. Or morphine: bushels and barrels of it without end. My poppy fields are vast beyond measure. You need never suffer the horrors of static reality again."

Outside the room, Holmes locked the door, his hand trembling ever so faintly as he twisted the key. He led me down the first flight of stairs, a finger to his lips. On the landing he stopped.

"We are out of earshot now, Watson. What is your opinion?"

"He is cruel enough to be whom he says he is. I should have smote him with my pistol for that despicable last remark."

"I meant about his timetable. Midnight is but four and one-half hours distant, and he has pledged to quit these premises today."

"I don't trust him, Holmes. Whatever devilry he has planned won't wait."

"I disagree. In his way he considers himself an honourable fellow. Tricksters never cheat. It robs them of their triumph."

"However did he know about the Milverton case?"

"That was a bit of a knockup, was it not? Milverton may have had a partner after all—either Smith, or one he's been in communication with. Smuggled intelligence is a parlour trick. Mind-readers and spiritualists have been using it for years. We shall ask him after the stroke of twelve. How long will Menitor sleep?"

"Until early morning, I should say."

"While he is incommoded, you are St. Poor's ranking medical authority. I advise you to place a guard upon Smith's door and another outside, at the base of the tower. I suspect our friend is too enamoured of his confidence skills to attempt anything so vulgar as an escape by force or an assault upon the bars of his window, to say nothing of the precipitous drop that awaits; still, one cannot be too careful. While we are waiting, I suggest we avail ourselves of the comforts of that public-house you mentioned earlier."

Holmes's expression was eager. It carried no hint of the irritable *ennui* he had worn to my consulting-room. Although I was loath to own to it, I had the Devil to thank for that, at least.

"You must think of it as if you'd borrowed from our century, and must repay the full amount," Holmes explained. "You would not return ninety-nine guineas and imagine that you had discharged your debt of one hundred. Therefore, you cannot consider that the twentieth century has begun until 1900 has come and gone."

We had enjoyed a meal of bangers-and-mash at our corner table, and were now relaxing over whiskies-and-soda; taking our time over the latter lest their depressant qualities rob us of reflexes we might need later that evening. Holmes had refused to discuss Smith since we had entered the public-house.

"I understand it now that you have explained it," said I, "but I doubt your example will prevent all London from attend-ing the pyrotechnics display over the Thames come the first of January."

"Appearances are clever liars; much like friend Smith."

I saw then that he was ready to return to the subject of our visit to Battersea.

"Is it your theory, then, that he is posing as a madman?"

"I have not made up my mind. Madmen lie better than most, for they manage to convince themselves as well as their listeners. If he is posing, we shall know once midnight has passed and he is still a guest of St. Poor's. A lunatic, once confronted with the evidence of his delusion, either becomes agitated or substitutes another for the one that has betrayed him. A liar attempts to explain it away. Conventional liars are invariably rational."

"But what could be his motive?"

"That remains to be seen. He may be acting in concert with an accomplice, distracting me from some other crime committed somewhere far away from this place to which we've been decoyed: Your position on the staff, and your reputation as my companion, may have given them the idea.

"Yes," he continued; "I think that scenario more likely than Smith enjoying making mischief and laying the guilt at Satan's door. Or such is my hope. In these times of temptation, any unscrupulous or lecherous man of the cloth is capable of the latter. I am no connoisseur of the ordinary."

"What do you think he meant when he spoke of Africa and Germany and America?"

"If I were Beelzebub, or pretending to be, I couldn't think of better places for calamity."

The publican announced that the establishment would be closing shortly. He was a narrow, rat-faced fellow, quite the opposite of the merry rubicund alesman of quaint English legend, and just the sort who would purchase provisions from a hospital orderly with no questions asked.

"What need for watches, when we have merchants?" Holmes enquired. "Shall we watch the patient in Room Six unfold his leathery wings and fly to the sound of mortals in torment?"

There was a different orderly at the door, built along the lines of a prizefighter, who held his truncheon as if it were an extension of his right arm. His predecessor had told him of our expected return. He reported that all was quiet. After a brief visit to Dr. Menitor's consulting-room to confirm that he continued to sleep soundly beneath the blanket I had spread over him, I rejoined Holmes, who had retained the key to John Smith's cell. I gripped my revolver as he unlocked the door.

Smith looked as if he had not moved in our absence. He sat with his hands resting on his thighs and his mocking smile firmly in place.

"How was the service?" he asked.

Holmes was unshaken by this assumption of our recent whereabouts.

"You're inconsistent. If you indeed saw into our minds, you would know the answer to that question."

"You confuse me with my former Master. I am not omniscient."

"In that case, the service was indifferent, but the fare above the average—surprising, in view of the proprietor's *laissez-faire* attitude regarding the source of his stock. We would have brought you a sample, but it might slow your flight."

Smith chuckled once more, in that way that chilled me to the bone.

"I shall miss you, Holmes. I am sorry my holiday can't be extended. I should have admired to snare your soul. I could build a new display with it in the centre."

"And to think only a few hours ago you offered me a seat at the head table."

"That offer has expired."

"Still, you exalt me. Dr. Watson is the better catch. He has the fairest soul in all of England, and the noblest heart."

Smith stroked his chin thoughtfully, as if he expected to find a spade-shaped beard there out of a children's illustrated guide to Holy Writ.

"I shall not be gone forever. If I return in a year, will you wager your friend's fair soul that I cannot vanquish you in a game of wits?"

"Twaddle!" I exclaimed; and looked to Holmes for support. But his reaction surprised and unnerved me. When he was amused, his own cold chuckle was nearly a match for Smith's. Instead, he appeared to grow a shade more pale, and raised a stubborn chin.

"You will forgive me if I decline the invitation," said he simply.

Smith shrugged. "It is one minute to midnight."

"You have no watch," I said.

"I told the time before there were clocks and watches."

I groped for the timepiece in my pocket, eager to prove him wrong, if only by seconds. Holmes stopped me with a nearly infinitesimal shake of his head. His eyes remained upon Smith. I clutched the revolver in my pocket, tightly enough to make my hand ache.

The first throb of Big Ben's iron bell penetrated the keep's thick wall.

"One minute, precisely," Smith said. "I don't pretend to think you will accept my word on that."

The bell bonged a second time; a third, fourth. We three remained absolutely motionless.

Upon the seventh stroke, the play of a cloud against the moon cast Smith's face in precise halves of light and dark, making of it a Harlequin mask. Still none of us stirred.

Eight.

Nine. The shadow passed; his visage was fully illuminated once again.

Ten.

Eleven. Another cloud, larger and denser than its predecessor, blotted out the light. The man seated on the cot was a figure drenched in black. I nearly squeezed the trigger in my confusion as to what he might be up to in the shadows. Only my old military training, and my long exposure to Holmes's own iron nerve, allowed me to hold my fire.

Came the final knell. It seemed to reverberate long after it had passed. Silence followed, as complete as the grave.

"Right." Holmes stirred. "Wake up, Smith. St. Walpurgis has fled, and you are still with us."

The moon now fell full upon the seated man. He raised his head. Relief swept through me. I relaxed my grip. Circulation returned tingling to my hand.

John Smith blinked, looked round.

"What is this place?" His gaze fell upon Holmes. "Who the devil are you?"

To this day, I cannot encompass the change that took place in the man in Room Six after Big Ben had finished his ageless report. He was still the same figure, fair and blue-eyed and inclining towards stout, but the mocking smile had vanished and his eyes had become expressive, as if whoever had decamped from them days before had returned. Most unsettling of all, his upper-class British accent was gone, replaced by the somewhat nasal tones of an American of English stock.

"Stop staring at me, you clods, and tell me where you've taken me. By God, you'll answer to Lord Penderbroke before this day is out. He's expecting me for dinner."

The young man's story would not be shaken, even when Holmes admitted failure and sent for Inspector Lestrade, whose brutish technique for obtaining confessions made up to a great extent for his shortcomings as a practical investigator. It was eventually corroborated when Lord Penderbroke himself was summoned and confirmed the young man's identity as Jeffrey Vestle, son of the Boston industrialist Cornelius Vestle, who had dispatched him to London to request the hand of his lordship's daughter in marriage and merge their American fortune with noble blood. Young Vestle had failed to keep a dinner appointment three days before, and the police had been combing the regular hospitals and mortuaries to determine whether he'd come to misfortune; private hospitals and lunatic asylums were at the bottom of the list.

Lestrade, in conference with Holmes and me in Dr. Menitor's consulting-room, was shamefaced.

"I daresay you have the advantage of me this one time, Mr. Holmes. The constables who brought the fellow here didn't recognise him from the description."

Holmes was grave.

"You won't hear it from me, Inspector. When the first stone is cast, you will hardly be the one it strikes."

Lestrade thanked him, although it was clear he knew not what to make of the remark, or of the grim humour in which it was delivered.

The mystery of the Devil of St. Porphyry's Hospital is a first in the matter that I was the client of record; but it is a first also in that I have chosen to place it before the public without a solution.

Dr. Menitor was satisfied, for with the departure of "John Smith," exited also the curse that seemed to have befallen his institution. He erased the mark from Nurse Brant's record and reinstated the temporarily larcenous orderly, assigning their lapses to strain connected with overwork, as he had dismissed his own emotional crisis, and thanked Holmes and me profusely for our intervention.

Holmes himself never refers to the case, except to hold it up as an example of *amnesia dysplacia*, a temporary loss of identity upon young Vestle's part, complicated by dementia, and brought on by stress, possibly related to his forthcoming nuptials.

"I might, in his place, have been stricken similarly," he says. "I met Penderbroke's daughter." But the humour rings hollow.

He considers his role in the affair that of a passive observer, and therefore not one of his successes. In this I am inclined to agree, but for a different reason.

I do not know that "John Smith" was the Devil, having left Jeffrey Vestle's body for a brief holiday from his busy schedule; I cannot say that Holmes's scientific explanation for the phenomenon—in which, I am bound to say, Dr. Menitor concurred—is not the correct one. I fervently hope it is. However, it does not explain how Smith/Vestle knew of the Milverton business, cloaked in secrecy as it was by the only two people who could give evidence (and never would, as to do so would lay us open to a charge of complicity in murder). At the time of that incident, the young Bostonian was three thousand miles away in Massachusetts, and in no position to connect himself with either Milverton or his fate. I am at a loss to supply such a connection, and too sensitive of Holmes's avoidance of the issue to bring it up.

Lack of evidence is not evidence, and such evidence as I possess is at best circumstantial.

Within months of Smith's leaving Vestle's body, the Bloemfontein Conference in South Africa came to grief over the British Foreign Secretary's refusal to back away from his political position and an ultimatum from Paul Krueger, the Boer leader, precipitating our nation into a long and tragic armed conflict with the Boers.

Less than two years later, on September 6, 1901, William McKinley, the American President, was fatally shot by a lone assassin in Buffalo, New York.

All the world knows what happened in August 1914, when Kaiser Wilhelm II invaded France, violating Belgium's neutrality and bringing Germany to war with England, and eventually the world. That prediction of Smith's took longer to become reality, but its effects will be with us for another century at least.

Regardless of whether Sherlock Holmes sparred with the Devil, or of whether the Devil exists, I know there is evil in our world. I know, too, that there is a great good, and I found myself in the presence of both in Room Six at St. Poor's.

For one fleeting moment, my friend put aside his pragmatic convictions and refused, even in jest, to gamble with Satan over my soul. I say again that he was the best and the wisest man I have ever known; and I challenge you, the reader, to suggest one better and wiser.

THE SERPENT'S EGG

(An unfinished Sherlock Holmes story)

uthor's Note: Many years ago, Jon Lellenberg and Martin H. Greenberg envisioned an ambitious project: a collaborative "round robin" Sherlock Holmes novel to which a group of established writers would contribute a chapter apiece. Ruth Rendell and Isaac Asimov accepted, among several others; but corralling disparate talents is one thing, getting them all to deliver on deadline another. As months and then years passed, the project faded away for lack of a complete manuscript. Fortunately, I drew the first spot, and can offer Chapter One without further preamble, for the first time in print. The title and concept are all mine.

I apologize for presenting a mystery without a solution: But perhaps the late Dr. Asimov, a prolific master of science fiction, may yet someday deliver his entry through a portal from the other world.

Throughout the score of years during which I assisted—and, I fear, far too frequently impaired—the efforts of my friend Sherlock Holmes to assemble the broken fragments of intelligence which came his way in the interests of curiosity and justice, I can count upon the fingers of one hand those occasions when he happened upon the singular circumstances by pure chance.

There was the grotesque affair of the Comte de Barzun's senility, the unexplained disappearance upon succeeding days of first one, then the other of the Pierpont twins in the London Underground, and the international sensations attending the murder of Lady Abigail Skinner and the marriage of the defrocked Bishop of Blackwell, neither of which was resolved to the satisfaction of either Holmes or the public.

He was, it must be noted, a *consulting* detective, and as success upon success mounted and his reputation grew beyond New Scotland Yard and our modest quarters in Upper Baker Street to encompass Buckingham Palace and all the great capitals of Europe, it was only natural that his cases should be brought to him rather than that he should venture out in search of them.

However, Holmes was no dilettante. While he may have refused the entreaties of a prince whose problem bore none of the intriguing points his intellect craved, he was not above imposing himself uninvited upon a situation whose features were sufficiently *outré* to draw him out of his occasional lethargy, without thought of personal gain. Such were the features presented by the terrifying and ultimately tragic adventure I have identified in my notes as The Salisbury Horror.

It began on a particularly fine day early in June 1896. The wind was blowing towards the harbour, carrying with it the choking yellow fog and the thousand reeks of four million souls, their beasts, and their great chugging and clamouring machines out to sea and replacing them with the sweet green scents of wood and meadow. It was a day calculated to make one rejoice in living, and consider reacquainting oneself with old comrades.

I decided I had neglected my friendship with Holmes for too long. Although the walk from the door of my club to his rooms was a long one, I turned away from the hansom cabs queued up along the pavement and struck off upon foot, swinging my cane and humming some nonsensical tune then popular among the music halls.

When I entered the sitting-room at 221B, Holmes was seated at his desk in his mouse-coloured dressing-gown, his long, spare form bent over an enormous ancient volume of the sort that in the years of our cohabitation had come in boxes to our door as regularly as eggs and milk. Others of their ilk had long since spilled beyond the confines of his presses and heaped the floor, indicating that the deliveries had not fallen off since my departure into marital territory. His austere features were frozen in a mask of intense concentration, and rather than disturb him, I made no greeting as I put up my hat and cane and fixed myself in my old armchair with that morning's edition of the *Times*.

"So Watson," observed he, after some little time had passed, "were you and Colonel Apperson successful in working out a more satisfactory conclusion to the Battle of Maiwand?"

"I fear not," I said. "His mind is of a military bent, and mine—"

Breaking off thus, I lowered the newspaper to stare at him across the top of his desk. His keen eyes bore the cold glow I had come to associate with the triumphal workings of his remarkable brain.

I crumpled the shipping columns in exasperation.

"Really, Holmes, I should think the Westminster theft a worthier recipient of your time than the business of following me about London and observing my activities for the mere purpose of a parlour trick."

"The Westminster theft was scarcely worthy of Inspector Lestrade. I resolved it over breakfast and sent my conclusions off to Scotland Yard by the morning post. Since then I have been at this desk, reacquainting myself with the idiosyncrasies of cuneiform and attempting to find merit in the current popular notion that patterns in crime are influenced by the phases of the moon. There is none, nor was there ever, at least as far back as Cyrus the Great." He slammed the book shut with a reverberating report and a cloud of yellow dust.

"How came you to know I was with Apperson, if you did not follow me?"

"By the grease upon your right coat-sleeve. The last time you thus defiled it was upon the twenty-ninth of April, when you stopped off at his rooms on your way to your club and wheeled him round the square in his bath-chair. He, or whoever looks after him in your absence, is evidently in the habit of over-lubricating the wheel nearest the brake, to the extent that anyone who leans forwards to release it must come away with a residue."

"Indeed. And what of your surmise that we were discussing Maiwand?"

"My dear fellow, you and Apperson *always* discuss that fateful conflict. Apperson is a Liberal and a teetotaler. Moreover, he does not gamble, and looks upon those who do as slaves to greed. Beyond the fact that you were both wounded at Maiwand, what else could you possibly find to talk about that would not result in a fit of fatal apoplexy for you both?"

My hand crept ruefully towards that old injury.

"You are a wizard, Holmes. I confess that I sometimes worry why you suffer me. My company must offer you no stimulation whatsoever."

"Quite the contrary. A garden cannot grow without compost." He sighed. "As things stand, my bed lies fallow. The current harvest of murderers and footpads all seem to have sprung from the same tired plot of ground. What I wouldn't give for a lone exotic orchid in that patch of onions."

I had seen him in this fug, but had seldom known him to belabour a metaphor to the point of absurdity.

"Perhaps you need fresh air. The air in here is as foul as Blackwall in November. Come with me upon a stroll."

"To what destination?"

"None in particular. I'm suggesting it for the exercise."

His great brow furrowed.

"I do not hold with this business of aimless locomotion to no useful end. The day will come when without warning you will require the energy you squandered scattering pigeons from your path."

"That is layman's fancy. As a physician, I can assure you that exercise increases endurance. As *your* physician, I strongly prescribe an outing. To remain cooped up on a salubrious day such as this is unnatural and unhealthy."

"Are you not expected on some domestic errand or other?" he asked petulantly.

"I am as free as the breeze. Mrs. Watson is engaged upon charity work all this week."

Further debate ensued, but whilst Holmes bowed to no one in matters of detection, his respect for my medical training was deeply seated in his regard for all things scientific. He knew as well that once I have expressed a conviction, I shan't be swayed from carrying it out.

At length, hatted and swinging our sticks, we found ourselves walking along Baker Street in the direction of George. The sun shone brilliantly and the folk of that busy thoroughfare were contentedly bustling about, the gentlemen sporting their best gaiters and patent-leathers, the ladies in their flowered hats with shopping baskets on their arms.

Holmes frowned when I ventured to comment upon the fine weather.

"I'm afraid that I cannot share your enthusiasm for bright days and fresh breezes, Watson. It is under just such conditions that the most loathsome things crawl from their holes. If you seek security and peace of mind, I offer you a driving rain and a plunging mercury every time. They are a lazy lot, these scoundrels, and admire their creature comforts."

"I should think they'd prefer to work under cover of darkness."

"You are not alone, but the statistics I've compiled argue against that conclusion. When I publish them, comparing shifts in criminal behaviour with changes in climate, the public will press the meteorological community to improve its atmospheric predictions, which if the campaign succeeds will prove a barometer for mayhem as well, infinitely superior to fancies concerning lunar gravity.

"Think of it, Watson!" he exclaimed. "A scientific plan for the prevention of crime. Here is Utopia indeed, without the pestiferous politics."

"But, Holmes," said I, "would that not also eliminate the necessity for your services as a detective?"

"Beyond doubt. It is the responsibility of any sincere researcher to answer all questions and therefore eliminate his profession."

I tried to contemplate a world with no use for Sherlock Holmes, but it all seemed like the novels of Monsieur Verne.

In the silence of our separate reveries we turned down Marylebone Lane. There my companion halted abruptly and grasped my arm in an oaken grip.

"Hullo, Watson! There is your cheery weather at its devil's work now."

We had stopped before a grey stone building of nondescript aspect, so much so that I was unaware of having seen it previously, despite countless excursions in that neighbourhood. It bore a tarnished plaque beside its entrance, identifying it as the headquarters of the British Retrospective Society, an organisation of which I had not heard. At the base of the stone steps leading up to the door, which yawned open, a pair of strangers were engaged in strenuous fisticuffs.

It was a sight common among the rough customers who prowled the sordid streets and alleys of the East End, but rare in our vicinity, and given the appearance of the combatants, sufficiently outside the ordinary to have drawn a small crowd.

The pugilists were attired as gentlemen, in frock coats and cravats, but there was little of the Marquess of Queensbury in the way they conducted their contest. As we watched, one man bit the wrist of the other, evidently attempting to persuade him to release the leather document case clamped in that hand. Blood trickled, but the portfolio remained in his desperate grip.

The biter was tall, black-bearded, and burly, tanned deep brown from prolonged exposure to a climate far less temperate than England's. The man holding the case, smaller and thin as a willow branch, was white-haired and sickly pale; a thick pair of rimless pince-nez swung free from a black ribbon clipped to a lapel.

All about them the street was littered with loose papers; I noted, almost humourously, that the efforts of the smaller man to defend himself were hampered by his unwillingness to give up his case, which he seemed unaware had tipped out all its contents in the struggle.

There was, however, nothing to laugh at in that ugly display. They punched, they grappled, they clawed at and clung to each other, and whilst it was obvious that the smaller man was losing the battle, it was equally evident that he would not give up even at the point of being beaten to death. Inexpertly he tried to fend off the blows raining upon him from a stronger and more experienced fighter, grimly determined to destroy him.

A fist the size of a Christmas ham came into contact with the smaller man's chin with a crack such as a billiard-cue makes upon the break. The recipient's eyes rolled over white and his knees buckled.

At this point, sensing victory, a fair man would have backed away. Instead, the big man stepped in closer and drew back his other fist for a blow that had death written all over it.

"Hold, sir! The fight is ended." Emphasising his point, Holmes laid his stick across that cocked arm.

Enraged by this interruption, the big man spun upon the stranger. Simultaneously the smaller man collapsed. I moved in swiftly to catch him before his head struck the pavement. He sagged heavily in my embrace.

"What affair is it of yours?" demanded the well-dressed ruffian, grasping Holmes's stick with his other hand.

"Murder is every man's affair," said he, as with a small but sudden exertion of his right hand he twisted the stick by its knob and with it the big man's wrist. In almost the same motion, he jabbed with his left, swept up his right elbow, snapping shut the fellow's jaws, and as the big man's face went slack stepped away to allow him room to fall. This he did, and no man came forwards to interrupt his descent.

The crowd broke into astonished applause.

Holmes ignored the accolade. "Is he badly injured?"

"I cannot say until I have examined him." Gently I lowered the smaller man to the ground.

Raising his stick, Holmes hailed a passing cab.

Within minutes we were back in Holmes's rooms, where my patient, deposited on the sofa, heaved a great sigh when I removed his collar, but had not yet regained his senses. I bathed his cheeks and forehead with cool water from a basin and, supporting his head with one hand, poured a small portion of restorative brandy between his parted lips. They were cracked and bleeding. I daubed at them with a damp cloth. He had a livid swelling above one eye and a bruise on his chin, but no bones were broken, and it was my prognosis that he would recover soon.

Holmes watched these procedures with one hand in his pocket and the other fingering the bowl of his clay pipe. He appeared not so much concerned with the patient's health as impatient to hear his story.

Suddenly the man's eyes opened wide and he made a motion to sit up. I checked it by laying a palm against his chest.

"My papers!" he said weakly. "Where are they?"

"Easy, my man," said I. "You've suffered a severe beating. You must lie still and rest."

"What good will that do without my life's work? I must have my papers!"

Holmes came forwards bearing the leather document case, no longer empty now but crammed near to bursting. It was a sturdy construction of brown calfskin that had once been fine, but which through age and misuse had grown shabby, stained, faded, and splitting at the seams.

"I trust everything is here," said Holmes. "I gathered every sheet I could find, but your condition seemed grave, and time was of the essence."

I doubt the man on the sofa heard the words. He'd no sooner laid eyes on the case than he shoved aside my staying hand and snatched the item from Holmes's grasp. In a trice he had the latch undone and was rummaging inside with both hands.

Little could be made of his muttering as he scanned each crumpled page through the pince-nez clutched in his fingers: I took it he was reading to himself in post-classical Latin. Certainly it was not the medical variety, as I understood not a word.

Holmes observed him throughout, as closely as the man was studying his precious sheets. So involved was he in concentration, the detective appeared not to notice that his pipe had gone out.

Presently our visitor fell back with a long, contented sigh, enfolding his case in both arms. He might have been its mother, and the case her child, snatched from beneath the wheels of a runaway carriage.

"Thank the Lord," said he, over and over. "Thanks be to the Lord."

"I should thank Him for more than the return of your papers," said I. "That brute we left in the gutter intended you should never leave it, except in a hearse."

He opened his eyes. "Oh, Ridpath is no brute. He's rigid in his convictions, but that's hardly uncommon. Had he lived during the Renaissance, he'd have asked Columbus if he had a pleasant voyage, and that would be the end of the matter. He combines the courage of David with the imagination of a postal clerk."

"Whereas you, Dr. H. Quicksilver Carlyle, are a man of both valour and vision."

"You flatter me, sir; though I may say in all humility that I have had my moments. I hope you will forgive me if I do not recall the circumstances of our introduction. That last blow must have rattled my medulla."

"No apology is necessary, Doctor. Since we have not met before this moment, it follows that we have not exchanged names."

A pair of thin white eyebrows lifted. "How, then, did you identify me? My name is not in these papers."

"Oh, but it is. I confess that I have a weakness for documents— a casualty of both our professions—and must read any that cross my path. Whilst retrieving the material that had strayed from your case, I chanced to note that they were written upon in Old English, albeit in a decidedly modern hand—and in pencil, which is an implement unknown in Beowulf's time.

"A transcription, then, scribbled—not in haste, which encourages slovenliness, but swiftly and with confidence—by one sufficiently familiar with that archaic and difficult tongue to scorn hesitation. Incidentally, it is my impression that those texts I paused to examine were something on the order of a chant or incantation. Mind you, I don't insist upon it. My own scholarship in the area is confined to crimes committed in pre-Norman England."

Holmes drew on his pipe, saw the fire had gone out, and relit it before continuing.

"As I returned the documents to their case, I noted that the flap bore the initials H.Q.C.: important information, which I placed in storage to be reclaimed later. All these observations took place in the time it took to rescue the papers and for the cab I'd hailed to come to a stop. More recently, during the good doctor's examination, I turned for information to a conceit of mine, the keeping of commonplace books into which I place all curious items that come my way. Under H—well, I shan't bother you with Hugh Capper, master of the doomed frigate H.M.S. *Delores*, or Henry Conk-Singleton, the forger. I was satisfied that you were neither. Elimination brought me at length to one name only."

Holmes picked up a book he'd left lying open in his chair, but he did not recite from it immediately.

"The *Times* was most amused by the disagreement between you and your colleague, Junius Ridpath, regarding the significance of excavations in the south of England. You read a paper to the British Retrospective Society expressing the opinion that the magical practices of Druidism, previously thought to have been introduced to the ancient Celts around

400 B.C., may in fact reach as far back as the New Stone Age, and represent the earliest religion known to man. Mr. Ridpath, currently serving as president of the British Retrospective Society, cleaves to the earlier assumption. I quote:

"'Dr. Carlyle has the qualifications of a master phrenologist. The researches of the great Copernicus would have been as nothing to Carlyle's claims that the sun revolves round the earth, on evidence discovered as providentially, and as mysteriously without supervision, as the scraps and shoddy he has placed before this body. Every quarter century or so, the science of antiquities must deal with this class of pest.'"

Holmes snapped shut the book. "It is the old story," he said. "The boor in the lecture-hall becomes a bully in the street. I was strongly inclined towards my identification of my friend's newest patient, and was gratified, when you mentioned Ridpath, to confirm it."

"A tour-de-force!" said I.

"A crass indulgence. I could simply have waited for Dr. Carlyle to come round and introduce himself, and spared the long-winded explanation of my methods."

"I should not have missed it for the bones of King Arthur." The eyes behind the archaeologist's spectacles glittered. "If you will permit me, I am not without resources of my own. You are, beyond doubt, Mr. Sherlock Holmes; and you, sir, are Dr. Watson, without whose pen I could not have connected the detection to the detective."

Holmes coloured slightly, and I laughed despite myself.

He shrugged then. "After all, you came to your misfortune just round the corner from Baker Street. How many detectives share the neighbourhood?"

"Surely the city is large enough to contain two close observers of evidence," said I, in the spirit of mollification.

Carlyle did not linger upon the subject, but became instantly serious.

"As a matter of fact, it was Ridpath's stand which compelled me to visit the Society once again, this time armed with all my notes. I encountered him in the foyer, hoping to challenge him to a formal debate before the membership. Instead, my latest findings threw him into a rage. He hurled me down the front steps, and followed me down with the intent of thrashing me.

"I fear you must supply the rest," he added. "I remember a great bursting light, such as the Aztecs of Mexico spoke of after days of ceremonial fasting, and then I can recall nothing until I awoke in this room."

"I shall waive the details and report that it will be a spell before Mr. Ridpath throws any more archaeologists down any more steps," said Holmes. "Your latest findings must have been inflammatory indeed."

"To some, perhaps; enlightening to others. I feel I can tell you, Mr. Holmes, that the combined intelligence of these papers and what I have seen with my own eyes will strip the veil from everything we do not know about ourselves and our civilisation."

Carlyle spoke in a quavering whisper. His eyes, naturally watery and somewhat protuberant, were bright as from fever. The tip of his short thin nose twitched like a rabbit's.

Holmes said, "Continue, but I beg of you to be brief."

Shy as he was, our guest's smile bordered upon sardonic. "In that case, I shall pass over the subject of everything we do not know."

Despite my protest, he swung his feet to the floor and, clutching his precious satchel in his lap, began the remarkable narrative I here relate.

"With the kind permission of Sir Cecil Chubb, who owns the property, I have been excavating among the ruins on the great Salisbury Plain in Wiltshire. Do you know the place, Mr. Holmes?"

"Not personally. I am aware that Stonehenge stands there."

"Precisely. Stonehenge. Pre-eminent among the megalithic monuments that tell us so much, and yet so very little, about our prehistoric ancestors. The great stones stand within a circular depression three hundred feet in diameter, with a broad roadway, inestimably ancient, leading up to it between steep embankments. The arrangement of the stones is orderly, the outermost series forming a circle enclosing a smaller circle, which in turn encloses a horseshoe."

As he spoke, Carlyle shifted his case onto the sofa beside him and cupped his hands, drawing an imaginary diagram of the concentric circles and half-circle. His palms, I noted, were thick with callus, unusual in a bookish scholar, but quite in keeping with his enthusiasm for his chosen field of study. Plainly he had not been able to resist shoveling dirt alongside his hired team of excavators.

"The innermost series, inside the horseshoe, will require further digging to reveal its shape. In my opinion, based upon my knowledge of the singular race that built it, it will resemble an egg. The stones are massive, suggesting both a great deal of sustained labour and at least a primitive understanding of engineering principles often attributed to Archimedes. To some of my colleagues, these are heresies, Mr. Holmes. They prefer their Greeks and Romans noble, their Stone Age artisans brutish and grunting. But I am satisfied as to my conclusions."

"I understand, Doctor. You are a lone voice in a wilderness peopled with Lestrades."

The sardonic smile flickered briefly. "Yes. I have read Dr. Watson's writings, and your assessment of the Inspector is known to me. I heartily agree with the comparison.

"Learned opinions vary regarding the construction's original purpose," he continued. "Some believe it is a combination sundial and calendar, tracking the hours of the day and the seasons of the year. Others maintain it is a monument to warriors slain in the defense of England against the Germanic invaders Hengist and Horsa. Still others hold it to be the ruins of a Roman temple.

"They are all mistaken," he concluded.

"And your proof?" enquired Holmes.

Carlyle patted his case.

"It is all here; the work of a lifetime. Old English manuscripts translated from Latin inscriptions based upon paintings found in caves as far away as Cornwall, their original artists gone to dust a thousand years before Christ. You think me less than hearty based upon my performance round the corner, yet I have crawled down burrows a ferret would shy from, shouted at mulish civil servants, and wrested precious papers physically from the clutches of illiterate housekeepers determined to use them to start fires. The science of antiquities is a savage business. More vigourous men than I have abandoned it for gentler pursuits. You may, in the light of this awareness, pardon my agitation when I announce that I, Hercules Quicksilver Carlyle, alone know the secret of Stonehenge."

I stifled a chuckle. I knew little about ancient England and cared less, but it amused me to think that this sallow and underfed ascetic had gone through life bearing the name Hercules.

In his concentration, Holmes appeared unmoved by my breach of manners.

"I hold false modesty and empty braggadocio in equal contempt," he told Carlyle, "and it's clear you're guilty of neither. It is wise, however, to consider one's audience first. Is this statement what led to your thrashing?"

"Yes. For all his reputation as an adventurer—he explored the Nile with Burton, and dove into Loch Ness in search of its Monster—Ridpath is a slave to convention. Give him a rhinoceros in full charge and he is happy. Speak to him of magic and mysticism and you will find in him no friend."

"Nor in me. I declare this world sufficiently challenging. I require no others."

Carlyle was undaunted. He leaned forwards, his eyes tiny suns.

"What if I were to tell you, Mr. Holmes, that magic existed in this very world you find so challenging, as far back as the dawn of man?"

"I should suggest you wait for the sun to rise higher, and your vision to improve."

"And what if I were to tell you that it exists still, here among our steam engines and electric dynamos?"

"I should request proof."

"What if I should withhold it?"

"I should demand it." Holmes traded his clay for his disputatious cherrywood and stuffed it with shag. "Cave paintings are absorbing relics, Doctor, but man is a simple creature, easily distracted. I would not place great faith in the records he has left behind. Even a down-to-earth fellow like Watson has known his flights of fancy. He publishes them upon a regular basis."

"I resent that, Holmes."

He waved a hand my direction, whether in dismissal or apology I could not say. His attention remained upon our guest.

"I do not speak of petroglyphs, Mr. Holmes. I am referring to the evidence of my own eyes. I have seen magic done at Stonehenge this very week."

My friend made no response. His pipe glowing, he deposited himself in his chair and stretched languidly, steepling his hands and blowing gales of smoke at the stained ceiling. His eyelids drooped. Knowing that this was the attitude he adopted when he was listening most keenly, I nodded reassuringly to Carlyle, who shrugged and continued.

"We know little of the Druidic cult beyond the accounts left to us by the Romans, who were naturally prejudiced against them," he said. "Where it began we may never know, but the fact that the Celts upon the continent sent their priests to England to undergo special training before the time of Caesar suggests strongly that its origins are here.

"The Druids were magi and are said to have practised the dark arts, which included rendering themselves transparent and transforming their bodies into all manner of shapes, both fixed and animate: trees, animals, rocks, running water. The early Christians believed they could—with Christ's permission—make rain, create fog, and draw fire from the sky. Saint Columba witnessed rituals in which a Druidic priest would stand upon one leg, point to the person upon whom a spell was to be laid, close one eye, and chant in a tongue unknown to the holy man. Various charms were employed in this process, most popularly the serpent's egg."

"What, no eye of newt?" Holmes spoke round his pipestem.

"You shan't shame me with laughter, sir. I have been jeered at by the most brilliant men of our day. The egg is significant. You will remember that I believe the center structure of Stonehenge to be egg-shaped. It is a symbol of birth, and of the fount from which life springs eternal. In that context we see it now at Easter, in children's brightly painted *ova*, but it was so revered many centuries before Christ. The charm itself was either a stone whose shape recalled that object or an actual fossilised egg, ancient even in the time of the earliest Druids, affixed to a chain or a thong and worn round the neck. Nothing can withstand its power."

"Twaddle," I said, beneath my breath. I'd come round to Holmes's point of view regarding our guest's character.

Carlyle heard, and turned his bright eyes upon me. "If you accept the Crucifixion and Resurrection as historical events, you are halfway in my camp. Fifteen hundred years closer to our time, the European explorers believed it as well, or there would be no Florida. Ponce de Leon set sail in search of eternal youth."

"He failed to find it," I pointed out.

"Understand, I shared your opinion when I started out. No longer is this the case.

"I have spent the past fortnight tenting on the Salisbury Plain with my crew of labourers, excavating by day, examining, cataloguing, and recording my discoveries by night. Nothing I found dissuaded me from my conviction that Stonehenge is both Druidic and prehistoric. Such evidence is material. I cannot explain in scientific terms what happened three nights ago.

"I was studying a shard of pottery in the light of a spirit-lamp, utterly absorbed in the delicate painting, when I suddenly became aware that I no longer required illumination to make out the details. My tent was flooded with light from outside.

"At first I believed the hour to be later than I'd supposed, and that in my concentration I'd passed an entire night into the dawn without noticing the time slipping away. However, my watch informed me it was only half-past two. It was still ticking; it had not stopped, and I'd never known it to lose more than a few seconds per day. Yet the light from without was growing brighter, and at a pace faster than ordinary sunrise.

"Emerging from my tent, I was dazzled by the glare, which filled the sky and threw grotesque crawling shadows upon the ground, extending weirdly from the base of the great monoliths. The sky was aflame, Mr. Holmes, with a fire such as this island has not seen since the great blaze that destroyed London in the time of our great-grandfathers. And there, no farther from me than that bow-window yonder, stood a singular figure."

"Man or woman?" Holmes enquired.

"The figure was hooded and its face was in shadow. However, as its height was nearer seven feet than six, my impression is that it was male."

"A seven-foot man is no less preposterous than a seven-foot woman." I'd dismissed the man as an inspired liar.

"Not so, Watson. I did a small service last year for a major who had brought back a Watutsi warrior from the Congo to serve as his batman. The fellow could scarcely have stood erect in this room." Holmes spoke quickly, evidently impatient to hear the rest of Carlyle's account.

"For the space of I know not how many minutes I watched that strange cloaked creature gyrating forth and back, swaying its arms and bobbing its head as though in the grip of some powerful drug. It was chanting in a high, ethereal voice, words which at length I recognised as an appeal in Old English to the dark gods who dwell in the wood and the water. His accent seemed otherworldly; but then those of us who study the language know it only as it was written. I cannot tell you the effect it had upon me, hearing a dead tongue come alive after nine hundred years."

I confess that at this point in the narrative I was rapt, no longer questioning its veracity, but caught up, as in a theatrical performance so well rehearsed as to annihilate the last lingering portion of doubt. I saw that mysterious chanting shade as clearly as Carlyle claimed it had appeared to him that night.

Of Holmes's reaction I had no hint. His pipe had gone dead, and with his hands folded now upon his breast and his eyes closed I would have thought he'd dozed off had I not known his habits and humours as well as I did.

The archaeologist seemed to have forgotten his audience. He went on speaking as if to himself, his myopic gaze fixed upon some point halfway between himself and his listeners.

"All at once the figure fell silent," said he. "It raised one foot, and supporting itself upon the other, pivoted round in a complete circle, coming to rest facing face foremost with a skeletal finger jabbed directly at me.

"I am a man of science, gentlemen, and yet I am not ashamed to say that at that moment I felt my marrow freeze. The reaction upon my hired labourers was stronger yet. They had all left their tents and were standing round me, entranced by the spectacle of that dancing phantom. Some were locals, for whom the practice of Druidism is modern and real. When that finger pointed, the group shouted and scattered, fleeing that place and leaving behind all their possessions. From that day to this I have not heard from any of them; not even to collect the wages they were owed."

"And the figure?" Holmes was visibly alert now, perched upon the edge of his chair like a man preparing to leap off a cliff. I had not observed him to move, though his physical attitude had changed completely.

The archaeologist moved his thin shoulders up and down. "Alas, I was distracted by the panic among the workmen. When I turned my attention back in that direction, the apparition was gone; vanished as if in a ball of smoke, for there was no place to hide in that flat depression in the earth."

Presently (to sum up the conclusion of Carlyle's account), the sky darkened, and soon the early morning was like any other in that desolate country, dreary and silent. He did not retire, but fetched his lamp and searched that place where the figure had stood. The ground was rock-hard. There was no physical trace of anyone having occupied it, then or later, when true daylight came. When hours later it became clear that his helpers had abandoned the site for good, he struck his tent and returned to London.

"You are the first, gentlemen, to hear my story," he said. "Ridpath would not listen."

Holmes sprang to his feet and rummaged through the stack of newspapers and other periodicals which upon inclement days filled the sitting-room and threatened to tumble onto the grate and catch fire. "Bah!" he exclaimed at last, and cast them aside.

"It has been raining heavily in Wiltshire for the past forty-eight hours, according to the *Times*," said he peevishly. "You are doubtless my superior in tracing the activities of a thousand years ago, Doctor, but very few are my equal in deciphering those of the past week. Unfortunately, rainfall is my *bête noire*. Were I upon that spot this very moment, I could see little more than you did when the event was fresh."

"My story is not yet complete."

The detective shifted his aggrievement from the weather to the scholar. "Very well, then: complete it. This is not a serial story in *The Strand*."

"I have not told you of the curse."

Holmes yelped and smacked his hands together. "Curse, yes! What is a ghost story without a curse?"

"You mock, but I would swear on my mother's grave what I have to say is true. I have told you that the magi dabbled in the black arts. Since the night that accusatory finger sought me out, I have had three near encounters with death. Yesterday morning, I stepped into Basil Street, a quiet thoroughfare, bent on visiting a colleague there, and was almost run down by a speeding four-wheeler. I was forced to dive for my life, and the wheels passed within inches of where I lay. Sir, the street was deserted when I stepped off the kerb."

"Carelessness."

"Late last night, a gas main exploded in front of the building where I live in Stepney. The blast tore a hole in the wall and destroyed my bed-chamber, which I had just left in order to fetch a drink of water."

"Faulty pipe."

"My fight with Ridpath is neither here nor there; he is quick to anger, but he would not kill a fly. The third incident took place as I approached Marylebone Lane this very afternoon. A pair of workers were raising a Louis XIV sideboard from the back of a wagon towards a first-floor window on Wigmore Street when the block-and-tackle failed. The massive piece of furniture plunged straight to the pavement, shattering into a hundred pieces not a handspan from where I was standing."

"Loose knot."

"Mr. Holmes, I am not accident prone. Surely so many life-threatening episodes in such a brief space of time is no coincidence."

Holmes shook his head.

"You are a fatalist, Dr. Carlyle. A horse bolts, a line breaks, a cupboard falls, and you think yourself marked for death. Yet here you sit, alive and according to a reliable physician in sound health. If you look at the situation from another point of view, you would say that you are blessed with extraordinarily good fortune."

"I fear the situation is quite the contrary. I consider myself a doomed man."

These words, and the expression upon the unhappy man's face, ended Holmes's ebullience. He bent and knocked his pipe against the grate.

"I am not unsympathetic," he said, straightening. "You will perhaps concur that half-past two on a dismal morning in a place like Stonehenge is scarcely a time for rational thought, particularly steeped as you were in the mystic rites of an ancient society. Absent the testimony of your hired help, who by your own admission are unavailable, you offer no evidence that what you think you saw actually took place. In fact, your unsuccessful quest for clues in the light of day knocks the foundation from under your claim."

Our visitor smiled, but this time there was no mirth in the twist of his thin lips.

"I am a seeker after truth, Mr. Holmes. You are one also, and so I think you will understand the need for an occasional falsehood when you are not quite prepared to share everything you have experienced. There *was* something on that plain. I found it within minutes of the vision's departure. I assure you I had been all over that ground over more than ten days and it was not there previously."

He reached inside his street-soiled shirt, and with a sudden exertion tugged loose something which had been tied round his neck.

Holmes and I leaned forwards, peering at the object he was holding for our enlightenment. From a rude leather thong hung an iron socket containing a smooth speckled object which caught the light upon its smooth surface, and which I took to be a fossilised egg.

ON THE
SIGNIFICANCE
OF BOSWELLS

his essay originally appeared as the introduction to *Sherlock Holmes: The Complete Novels and Stories*, published in two volumes by Bantam Books in 1986. It reflects my personal sentiments about the importance of Dr. Watson to the Canon; and I'm pleased to report that the entertainment industry has come round to my way of thinking in the way he's now portrayed on TV and in the movies. This version has been revised to address a twenty-first-century audience, with background on the original Holmes series excised as extraneous and new material added.

I submit for your inspection one John H. Watson: medical man, late British Army surgeon, raconteur, journalist, connoisseur of women, Knight of the Battered Tin Dispatch-Box, valiant and loyal friend.

He has suffered mightily at the hands of scholars and the public since the 1887 appearance of *A Study in Scarlet* in *Beeton's Christmas Annual*, calumniated on the one hand as a tanglefooted incompetent and on the other as a boozy Bluebeard, to say nothing of sundry slanderous impostitures his admirers have been forced to endure, beginning in 1905, when Sherlock Holmes and his indispensable biographer made their silent-screen debut. (For the purposes of this essay, we will ignore the 1900 vignette *Sherlock Holmes Baffled*, in which Watson was ungraciously not invited to appear.) Chief among these poseurs was the otherwise distinguished character actor Nigel Bruce, whose corpulent and ineffectual bumbler in thirteen Universal features starring Basil Rathbone in the 1940s fixed Watson in the public mind for decades as a comic foil.

It was an ill-advised comedown from the first two features pairing Basil Rathbone's Holmes with Bruce's physician, *The Hound of the Baskervilles* and *The Adventures of Sherlock Holmes*, both released by Twentieth-Century Fox in 1939. Watson's dunderheaded side was more subdued, and he was even of assistance in the cases' successful resolution. They were also the first films to set the stories during the Victorian era. Prior to that, Holmes and Watson were presented as contemporaries with the producers and audiences—which in many cases they were, cast so recently after the turn of the twentieth century. The decision, when the series moved to Universal, to catapult the duo into a World War II setting, substituted a schleppy bucket hat for Holmes's iconic deerstalker and addled Watson's brain. The fore-and-aft cap would return in short order, but the faithful companion took decades to recover.

If a mop bucket appeared in a scene, Bruce's foot would be inside it, and if by some sardonic twist of fate and the whim of director Roy William Neill (the bold auteur behind *Frankenstein Meets the Wolfman*) he managed to stumble upon an important clue, he could be depended upon to blow his nose in it and throw it away. It's most fortunate that this healthcare giver spent more time in a hansom cab racing toward some mysterious venue than treating patients in an examination room. I am convinced that this lampoon of Holmes's trusty right bower has colored much of the psuedoscholarship undertaken during the past sixty years regarding the good doctor's life and habits.

Moriarty was not involved in this deceit; it was made without malice. Directors simply don't know what to do with Watson. His presence in fifty-six of the sixty published adventures (two are told by a third-person narrator, and Holmes himself relates "The Adventure of the Lion's Mane" and "The Adventure of the Blanched Soldier") is crucial, for he is both the storyteller and the buffer between the cold, blinding light of Holmes's intellect and the reader. On stage and screen he is a fixture, and directors abhor characters who don't appear to be doing anything. Since much of the action—and, despite the claims of some proponents of the American school of detective fiction, there is plenty of action in the Sherlock Holmes series—takes place in the final scenes, the simplest solution is to provide a number of banana skins for Watson to take a Brodie on until his brawn is required. Besides, it makes Holmes look that much smarter and pleases the groundlings.

Watson was the first to confess that his friend's analytic mind worked on a plane he himself could scarcely conceive, and although in *The Hound of the Baskervilles* he pokes some good-natured fun at himself for fancying he has mastered the science of deduction in the matter of Dr. Mortimer's stick, he never pretended to skills beyond his own considerable ones. Unlike most of his antecedents in the ape world of mystery fiction, he never prolonged or spoiled a case by bungling. Indeed, time and again, in such tight situations as the long-awaited encounter with the spectral hound on the Baskerville common and that magnificently suspenseful chase down the Thames in *The Sign of Four*, he quite saved the day for the often impetuous Holmes with his courage and propensity toward action at the precise moment it is needed. "I am lost without my Boswell," declares Holmes in "A Scandal in Bohemia"; and it's probable that, in his supreme egocentricity, he is not fully aware of the statement's truth.

Holmes, of course, was the star, and disregarding Watson's close physical and spiritual resemblance to the dashing Richard Harding Davis of Hearst's *New York Journal*, Watson was not the sort of journalist who makes himself the hero in his dispatches. Yet, guileless chronicler and respecter of privacy that he was, we know rather more about him than we do about his companion.

In *Scarlet*, he refers modestly to his service with the Berkshires at Maiwand, touching almost apologetically upon the severe wound he received there that troubled him throughout his life—and not just physically, for we may infer from his inability in later years to recall whether the jezail bullet passed through his leg or his shoulder that his conscious mind attempted to wipe out all memory of the incident. Maiwand was a major British defeat, in which nearly half its force was slain, wounded, or reported missing after its clash with a hugely superior force of Afghans. We learn of Watson's near-fatal bout with infection ("enteric fever"), his lack of family, and the alarming state of his finances, and all before he makes contact with Sherlock Holmes.

(On what became of the "bull pup" that he told Holmes he kept, we can only speculate, and various conjectures about colonial slang for "bad temper" and the existence somewhere of a bastard son seem both unsatisfying and actionable. It was refreshing, in 2009's enormously successful film *Sherlock Holmes,* to find Jude Law's Watson in possession of a full-grown English bulldog: The researchers did their homework.)

We become aware also, counter to the Oliver Hardy image projected by Hollywood, that at this time Watson is "as thin as a lath and as brown as a nut," and although by the time of the morally unsettling "Adventure of Charles Augustus Milverton" he will be described as "a middle-aged, strongly built man—square jaw, thick neck, a moustache," this early picture certainly challenges the common conception.

What emerges, then, be he lean and tan or broad and brawny, is a figure both distinctive and arresting, more Nick Carter than Sancho Panza, and strongly attracted to women, who in turn find him attractive. Holmes makes note in "The Resident Patient" of his friend's "natural advantages" in that department, and in *The Sign of Four* Watson himself uncharacteristically boasts of "an experience of women which extends over many nations and three separate continents"—driving subsequent scholars into frenzied debate over which was the third continent. He is often observed admiring a clean feminine profile or a trim ankle, and his memory for the details of a handsome female client's dress rivals Holmes's more practical one. But he is no callous swordsman and commits himself willingly to the chains of matrimony when the lovely Mary Morstan beckons in *Four.*

Which brings us to the other extreme: that brand of canard, born of supposition and sexual frustration masquerading as scholarship, concerning Watson's marriage(s). We hear first of his bereavement in "The Adventure of the Empty House"; then, in "The Adventure of the Blanched Soldier," dated nine years later, Holmes alludes querulously to his friend's desertion of him for a wife. The obvious conclusion is that he remarried; but this is not sufficient for some trash pickers who have published learned treatises in distinguished periodicals attesting to a third, fourth, and even a *fifth* marriage, including one before the seminal events described in *Scarlet*. I relegate all this into the same bin with the speculations regarding Watson's drinking habits because he mixed up a few dates and references in a forty-year chronicle and wonder that the man who applauded his friend Sherlock Holmes for his intention to horsewhip a cad in "A Case of Identity" has not come out of seclusion before this to defend his name before a magistrate.

Considerable sanctimony has been employed as well in denigrating his skills as a doctor. This is based on the evidence of emergency first-aid procedures that were quite rightly presented in layman's terms to avoid overloading the narrative with scientific jargon, and a reference in "The Red-Headed League" to a practice that was "never very absorbing." To this we need only respond that he never lost a patient in our presence who was not already beyond the reach of medicine. "Do you imagine," says Holmes, in "The Adventure of the Dying Detective," "that I have no respect for your medical talents?" His ethics have been called into question for his readiness to abandon patients on the slightest notice and run off with Holmes on some new quest. Admittedly, the energetic veteran of the bloody Afghanistan campaign was too adventurous for the staid life of office hours and regular rounds. But Drs. Anstruther and Jackson were close by and ever eager to assume his practice while he was away.

Watson was a swashbuckler. There is no use denying it, even if denial were necessary. He braved poisoned darts in *The Sign of Four*, dispatched the devil-dog to save Sir Henry's life in *The Hound of the Baskervilles*, scaled a wall with the police hard on his heels in "The Adventure of Charles Augustus Milverton," and at the time of "His Last Bow," when he was well past sixty, offered his surgical skills to his country on the eve of World War I. (That they were accepted should lay to rest once and for all any questions about their merit.) Notwithstanding his friend's mastery of boxing and fencing, and sitting-room marksmanship that would quicken the heart of an Annie Oakley, when a pistol was necessary it was Watson who carried it, at Holmes's request. A modern-day police officer could do far worse in a partner, and often does.

Mind, the man had faults. Along with the standard Victorian irritability and a tendency, displayed as early as *Scarlet*, to dismiss those things about which he knew nothing as "ineffable twaddle," the most destructive of these seems to have been his gambling. He confesses ruefully to Holmes in "The Adventure of Schoscombe Old Place" that he has paid for his knowledge of racing with "about half my wound pension," and in "The Adventure of the Dancing Men" we learn that his checkbook is locked safely away in Holmes's desk, a self-protective measure familiar to compulsive gamblers who recognize their weakness.

"Eureka!" exclaim supporters of the many-times-wedded theory; a clue at last to the cause of the dissolution of his marriages. Yet it should be noted that in that same adventure he has resisted the urge to invest in the "sure thing" of South African securities, and that by "His Last Bow" he has sufficiently conquered his problem to engage in the rich man's sport, in 1914, of driving an automobile.

The daily double, perhaps. But at its worst, the lure of games of chance appears to be a placebo for his adventurous soul—a substitute in quieter times, like Holmes's own darker habit, for the adrenaline rush of hansom-cab chases through Soho and midnight stakeouts in Dartmoor. The vice is less insidious than cocaine addiction; and let us not forget that if Holmes helped out Watson by withholding his funds, Watson succeeded single-handedly in weaning his friend away from the needle.

And Watson grew. While Holmes the rheumatic beekeeper on the South Downs is not significantly less idiosyncratic than Holmes the young criminologist at Bart's, Watson is not the same person when we leave him as when we made his acquaintance. The roommate who scores verbally off a more than usually truculent Holmes at the beginning of *The Valley of Fear* could or would not have done so as recently as "The Adventure of the Solitary Cyclist," when a withering evaluation of his research efforts near Surrey renders the detective piqued and quarrelsome. Although several of Watson's conclusions regarding the identity and character of Dr. Mortimer based upon his stick in *Hound* are erroneous, as many are correct: The invalided surgeon in *Scarlet* who threw down "The Book of Life" because he found deduction based on analysis unacceptable would not have been capable of that.

Watson at the end of the Canon is a father confessor, tolerant of human frailty, and well aware of his limitations, while Holmes's consistent refusal to acknowledge his own reduces him to an oddity, albeit a fascinating and brilliant one. Which man you will invite for dinner depends upon the personality and temperament of the other guests.

From the outset a man who walked with kings—the late Bohemian monarch springs to mind—yet never lost the common touch—yellow-backed novels and the sea stories of William Clark Russell remained among his reading pleasures—Watson was the ballast upon whose reassuring weight Holmes came to rely more and more as the gaslight era drew to a close. That was the basis of the partnership from March 1881 to August 1914, and those who suggest homosexuality, as they have of every other famous male team from Wyatt Earp and Doc Holliday to Batman and Robin, either are ignorant of the largely masculine character of late nineteenth-century English society or are unable to accept Holmes's notorious misogyny at face value.

The stories without Watson, or in which he plays a minor role, are arid and disappointing, lack humanity, and embarrass one with Holmes's unchained narcissism. They are self-conscious and help to propagate the disturbing rumour that Sherlock Holmes and Dr. Watson never existed, and that they were the creations of Sir Arthur Conan Doyle, who wrote about the Boer War and Professor Challenger, introduced the sport of skiing to Switzerland, and conducted seances with Houdini's ghost. This is never the case when Holmes and Watson are in their proper places as detective and biographer, or even during Holmes's absences, as when Watson gets his chance to play the bully hero in chapters 6 through 11 of *Hound*.

I prize that story above all the others, in part because of Watson's free rein. Delivered from Holmes's shadow, this visitor to Devonshire is gallant, fearless, impeccably well-mannered, and a strong shoulder for the troubled young baronet to lean upon, emotionally and physically. He's the perfect houseguest. Were the situation reversed, and Holmes in residence sans Watson, the detective might find his bags packed and waiting for him in the entrance hall after three days, mystery or no.

Above all, Watson has the virtue of self-effacement. He allows himself to appear less astute than the reader, rendering himself more approachable than the aloof and awesome Holmes, without sacrificing respect for his native intelligence. The thinness of this particular highwire is best appreciated when someone falls off—a frequent occurrence among those who have attempted to duplicate the stunt. Said the detective, sorely missing his friend's assistance in "The Blanched Soldier": "A confederate who foresees your conclusions and course of action is always dangerous, but one to whom each development comes as a perpetual surprise, and to whom the future is always a closed book, is indeed an ideal helpmate."

In recent years, the best and bravest companion any detective ever knew has fared better on the big and small screens. Two different takes on Holmes vs. Jack the Ripper, 1965's *A Study in Terror* and 1979's *Murder by Decree*, gave us Donald Huston and James Mason, respectively, and David Burke and Edward Hardwicke took turns balancing out Jeremy Brett's nervous, arrogant Holmes in the Thames Television series of the 1980s. In 1976, Robert Duvall, one of the best actors of his generation, immersed himself in a stirring, sympathetic role opposite a manic Nicol Williamson in *The Seven-Percent Solution*. These were intelligent and sensitive characterisations, involving bouts of heroism and masculine charm, and any of them could have sustained a long and loyal relationship with the eccentric sleuth. But it took a new century and a new kind of moviemaking to give us Watsonians what we'd craved from the beginning.

Critics who had obviously been reared on Nigel Bruce dismissed Jude Law as "too pretty" for the role, unaware that until "Charles Augustus Milverton," one of the last entries in the series, when the character was well into middle age, he had never been described in detail. Certainly, internal evidence regarding his popularity with women suggest dash, personality, and a pleasing figure and countenance: a hunk, in postmodern terminology. And he is a man of action, a fit partner for Holmes the fencer, prizefighter, and practitioner of martial arts. When we first see Law in *Sherlock Holmes*, he is seated in a Black Maria in full gallop beside Lestrade, buzzing the cylinder of a loaded revolver in the Wild West tradition; within moments, he's flattening henchmen with his fists and coolly swapping lead with killers. More than once he saves Holmes's life, when he isn't sniping at his friend's annoying eccentricities. This is no overstuffed geezer, ducking his head and smiling cherubically at a condescending pat on the head from his master.

Sherlock Holmes: A Game of Shadows followed in 2011, with all the same counters in place (as well as the delicious wrestling match between Holmes and Professor Moriarty atop the boiling Reichenbach Falls, accompanied by whole snatches of narrative and dialogue taken straight from the Canon). Both films were huge commercial successes, and more are promised.

This first big franchise of the third millennium was advertised, and accepted by reviewers, as a "reimagining" of the Canon, but there is nothing here that was not there from the beginning. Holmes and Watson were the predominant action heroes of the horse-and-buggy era. When they were discovered by Hollywood, the "buddy picture" was born.

If there is a Valhalla for superhuman sleuths and their all-too-human compatriots, it will allow them freedom at night to leap aboard a hansom in the fog and provide them a cosy cluttered place by day to feast upon cold fowl, whiskies-and-soda, and tales from Watson's storied tin box. If the detective should suffer overmuch from the artistic temperament, and his fellow-lodger should dwell overlong upon the fairness of a wrist or the timbre of a feminine voice, so much the better, for us and them. Literature never produced a relationship more symbiotic, nor a warmer and more timeless friendship.

WAS SHERLOCK HOLMES THE SHADOW? (A TRIFLE)

There is nothing so important as trifles.
—Sherlock Holmes

his essay represents my sole contribution to *The Baker Street Journal*, the late great publishing organ of the Baker Street Irregulars. Named after Holmes's unofficial spy network of street urchins, the BSI is a national organization whose members meet in regional groups throughout America and at an annual banquet in New York City to discuss and celebrate the lives and adventures of Sherlock Holmes and John H. Watson, and whose pleasant conceit is that the pair are historical figures, not creatures of fantasy. The piece appeared in the March 1982 number. It's an affectionate takeoff on learned discourse in general, which is a hallmark of the BSI. It has not been in print in thirty years.

While paging through Walter B. Gibson's fascinating potpourri, *The Shadow Scrapbook* (New York: Harcourt Brace Jovanovich, 1979), which recounts the career of that dark avenger who for twenty-five years kept audiences glued to their radio sets to find out "what evil lurks in the hearts of men," I was struck by the resemblance of The Shadow as depicted by various illustrators to another avenger whom we all know and admire.

Between the black slouch hat and cloak was that same hawklike profile which, reproduced in wax and cast upon a drawn blind, caused Colonel Sebastian Moran to expend both a bullet and his freedom in the spring of the year 1894. Equally as prominent were the piercing gray eyes, bushy brows, and tightly pressed lips so suggestive of a red Indian. Sidney Paget, the man whose pen-and-ink drawings in *The Strand* magazine set the pace for all representations of Sherlock Holmes to follow, and Tom Lovell, whose artistic talents graced the pages of *The Shadow* magazine for many years, might have been working from the same model.

I thought little of this at the time. Similarity of features is hardly conclusive evidence, and wasn't The Shadow a fictional character created by Gibson writing under the pseudonym of Maxwell Grant, later to find greater fame through the media of radio and the screen?

But hold. What was this item reproduced from the very first story, "The Living Shadow"?

*This is to certify that I have made careful
examination of the manuscript . . . as set down by Mr.
Maxwell Grant, my raconteur, and do find it a true
Account of my activities upon that occasion. I have
therefore arranged that Mr. Grant shall have exclusive
privilege to such further of my exploits as may be
considered of interest to the American public.
The Shadow*

Who was The Shadow? In *The Shadow Unmasks*, he is said to have been famed aviator Kent Allard, lost and presumed dead when his plane went down over the Yucatan Peninsula years before, although Grant made the same claim about millionaire Lamont Cranston, only to reveal later that Cranston was just another of the many guises The Shadow assumed to continue his war on crime. Accepting The Shadow's existence (for who can prove a negative?), it seems probable that the chronicler's subject supplied him with equally false information regarding Allard in order to protect his own identity.

Physical appearance having been dealt with, what are the other "handles" by which we may hope to grasp the secret?

1. Wrote Gibson/Grant, in Otto Penzler's *The Great Detectives* (Boston: Little, Brown and Co., 1978): "The most inimitable of The Shadow's features was his laugh, which could be weird, eerie, chilling, ghostly, taunting, mocking, gibing, sinister, sardonic, trailing, fading, or triumphant." In *The Hound of the Baskervilles*, Watson, writing of *his* hero, stated: "He burst into one of his rare fits of laughter. . . . I have not heard him laugh often, and it has always boded ill to somebody."

2. The Shadow was a master of disguise, with "the ability to assume new identities with chameleon rapidity." This talent enabled him to counterfeit the appearance and actions not only of financiers Cranston and George Clarendon, but also of various denizens of the underworld, so well that he could infiltrate their ranks without suspicion. Holmes's felicity in this area is legendary, as his "very soul seemed to vary with every fresh part that he assumed."

3. In his youth, The Shadow journeyed to the Orient, where he acquired, among other things, "the power to cloud men's minds." Holmes spent most of his Reichenbach-induced hiatus in the East, where he amused himself "by visiting Lhassa, and spending some days with the head lama. . . . passed through Persia, looked in at Mecca, and paid a short but interesting visit to the Khalifa at Khartoum." Later, Watson made mention of his friend's "almost hypnotic power of soothing," and confessed upon more than one occasion to a sensation of dullness in the presence of the great man's brilliance.

4. An expert shot with either hand, The Shadow displayed his marksmanship time after time against overwhelming odds with an automatic pistol in each hand. Certainly it would have been no feat for him to accomplish Holmes's "patriotic V.R." in bullet-pocks on the wall of the sitting-room at 221B.

5. Returning to physical description, a contest held among The Shadow's many fans during the 1930s, in which clues to the identity of the Knight of Darkness were passed over the airwaves, established him as tall and slender: two of Sherlock Holmes's most striking physical characteristics.

6. Despite his spare physique, the great detective possessed exceptional strength, which allowed him to perform such stunts as the straightening of the fireplace poker twisted by the villainous

Dr. Roylott in "The Adventure of the Speckled Band." Holmes's "grasp of iron" is mentioned in "His Last Bow." In *The Living Shadow*, would-be suicide Harry Vincent was saved from a plunge off a high bridge by "an iron grip" that lifted him back onto a solid footing "as though his body possessed no weight whatever."

7. The term most often employed in describing The Shadow's purpose is that of "avenger," likening him to a fierce angel sent straight out of the Old Testament to punish evildoers. Similarly, Holmes once said, "I am the last court of appeal," and, in "A Case of Identity," resorted to the threat, if not the actual intention, of smiting a particularly disagreeable adversary with a riding crop.

WAS SHERLOCK HOLMES THE SHADOW?

Is it just a coincidence that the dark punisher made his first appearance shortly after Holmes took "His Last Bow"? There is, of course, a question of age, as the Canon indicates that at the time of The Shadow's entrance in 1930 the Victorian detective would have been seventy-six, hardly capable of the exploits assigned this swashbuckler. But are we to believe that the royal jelly derived from Holmes's bees would prolong his life without extending the properties of youth? Would he have bothered to partake of it if it could not, like Fu Manchu's *elixir vitae*, be expected to retard the aging process in order to spare his great mind the horrors of dissolution? It's a reasonable theory at least, and far more of an explanation than either Holmes or Watson offered for this bizarre choice of hobbies in retirement.

Granted, The Shadow's methods are not those of the Sherlock Holmes we know. But the Master was always ahead of his time, making use of the latest advances in criminal scientific research—indeed, in devising his own—while Scotland Yard bustled about photographing murder victims' retinas in hopes of lifting images of their assailants. As more law enforcement units adopted his strategy, is it so inconceivable that he would advance yet another step, the better to stay ahead of his opponents? New York City having replaced London in importance, would he not contemplate a change of scenery, secure in the knowledge that to the world at large he was enjoying a life of meditation and apiculture on the South Downs? Would not the experience gained from Sherlock Holmes's war with Professor Moriarty aid The Shadow in his never-ending struggle against Shiwan Khan, lineal descendant of Genghis, who plots to rule the world?

Was it coincidence that Orson Welles's voice was heard over the ether as both The Shadow and Sherlock Holmes? Or was it a mocking clue dropped by the man who returned the naval treaty to a distraught Percy Phelps in a covered dish?

Accents are immaterial. Holmes had disguised his voice before, to suit his various masquerades. Should professional assistance be required, not all the voice coaches of the Broadway stage were in Hollywood, helping former silent-screen stars improve their diction to suit the era of sound. They could train the others in his circle to trade their crisp *t*'s and short *a*'s for the broader Yankee pronunciation.

Could Watson have been the mysterious Burbank, who relayed The Shadow's instructions to his nameless ring of adherents? Could they have been the adult counterpart of the Baker Street Irregulars? Was the lovely Margot Lane, Lamont Cranston's confidante and The Shadow's female accomplice, Irene Adler? Could thickset, sedentary desk man Claude Fellows have been Mycroft, persuaded to abandon the Diogenes for Cranston's and Clarendon's exclusive Cobalt Club? Or are we straying too far?

Only The Shadow knows.

SUGGESTED READING

he best source, of course, is the original. For those who know Sherlock Holmes only through the many adaptations of his adventures, or the thousands of tributes and pastiches written by other authors, I recommend Sir Arthur Conan Doyle's *A Study in Scarlet*, *The Sign of Four*, *The Adventures of Sherlock Holmes*, *The Memoirs of Sherlock Holmes*, *The Return of Sherlock Holmes*, *The Case-Book of Sherlock Holmes*, *His Last Bow*, *The Hound of the Baskervilles*, and *The Valley of Fear*; for those who know him already from these books, I recommend a return visit. They're as enchanting the twentieth time round as they were the first.

A complete bibliography of writings *about* Holmes would command as many volumes as the *Oxford English Dictionary*, and more than most lifetimes. He has been written about more than any other character in literature, including Hamlet and

Don Quixote, and more material appears by the day. The following is a limited listing of some of the best that have come my way. They have all been of immense help in all my writings about the world's greatest detective and his loyal partner.

Baring-Gould, William S., ed. *The Annotated Sherlock Holmes*. New York: Clarkson N. Potter, 1967.

Baring-Gould dedicated much of his life to Sherlockian scholarship, and this is the end result, a massive two-volume compilation of all the stories and novels in the Canon, arranged chronologically in the order in which the cases occurred (as opposed to order of publication; a Homeric effort of internal and external reasoning), with sidebars and footnotes provided by hundreds of the editor's colleagues, and reproductions of the original illustrations that accompanied the stories. It's a treat for old-school aficionados and fresh converts alike, the ideal pastime for an inclement weekend when the wind "sob(s) like a child in the chimney."

Baring-Gould, William S. *Sherlock Holmes of Baker Street*. New York: Bramhall House, 1962.

This is a delightful biography of Holmes, citing numerous references in the Canon for its speculations on the life and times of the world's first consulting detective, and a fitting preparation for Baring-Gould's magnum opus (see above).

Bullard, Scott R., and Collins, Michael Leo. *Who's Who in Sherlock Holmes*. New York: Taplinger, 1980.

What it says it is, concentrating upon the clients, witnesses, victims, and villains who crossed Holmes's path.

Carr, John Dickson. *The Life of Sir Arthur Conan Doyle*. New York: Harper & Row, 1949.

One of the first, and still the best, of Conan Doyle's many biographies. Carr, who collaborated with (some say ghosted for) Arthur's son Adrian on *The Exploits of Sherlock Holmes*, provides a thorough, respectful, and enormously readable take on one of the most popular writers in history, with insight into the sources of his inspiration. The biographer makes the case that Conan Doyle's simultaneous championship of rational thought and embrace of spiritualism were entirely consistent with his character.

Hardwick, Michael and Mollie. *The Sherlock Holmes Companion*. New York: Bramhall House, 1962.

One of the first encyclopedic references to the characters, events, and settings employed in the stories. An entertaining read as well as a life- and time-saver for scholars and pasticheurs. The Hardwicks spent hour upon hour poring through the Canon so we don't have to.

Harrison, Michael. *In the Footsteps of Sherlock Holmes*. New York: Drake, 1976.

What was significant about Fleet and Harley streets? Where is Covent Gardens, and what do they grow there? Can one still get a meal at Simpson's? These questions and hundreds more are answered here. A fine guide to have on your desk, or under your arm during a walking tour of London. Harrison walked it, you can be sure.

Park, Orlando. *Sherlock Holmes, Esq., & John H. Watson, M.D.: An Encyclopedia of Their Affairs*. Evanston, IL: Northwestern University, 1962.

Until Jack Tracy's exhaustive reference appeared (see below), the existence of "dueling encyclopediae" helped to fill in certain gaps found in one or the other. I still recommend Orlando and the Hardwicks for their slightly different cataloguing procedures, which together provide direct access to certain elusive details. (Reprinted in trade paper by Citadel as *The Sherlock Holmes Encyclopedia* in 1981.)

Rosenberg, Samuel. *Naked Is the Best Disguise*. New York: Bobbs-Merrill, 1974.

I'm not sure whether Rosenberg's written a satire of literary scholarship in general or is dead serious about his assertions. He draws a fuzzy parallel between Mary Shelley's *Frankenstein* and the life of Friedrich Nietzche, but for the life of me I don't see what they have to do with each other, or for that matter what either of them has to do with Sherlock Holmes. But watching the author leap from one absurd conclusion to the next is great fun, like watching a clown shot from a cannon into a vat of Reddi-Wip.

Starrett, Vincent. *The Private Life of Sherlock Holmes*. Chicago: University of Chicago Press, 1960.

Not to be confused with Billy Wilder's clever film of the same name (and which gives us not a bad Watson in Colin Blakely), Starrett's was the first Holmes biography, as well as one of the first to treat a character generally regarded as fictional as if he really lived. The book raises and answers many of the questions that still interest Sherlockians, and may have been the catalyst that created the Baker Street Irregulars, with the inspiration of the older Sherlock Holmes Society of Great Britain. It's as much fun to read (and reread) as Conan Doyle's stories themselves. (WARNING: This book contains material that may turn the reader from a casual fan into a diehard Holmes fanatic. It did me.)

Tracy, Jack. *The Encyclopedia Sherlockiana*. Garden City, NY: Doubleday, 1977.

This is the be-all and end-all of its kind: Everything you always wanted to know about the stories and novels, organized alphabetically and with an eye towards swift access between two covers, with illustrations and photographs. It appeared while I was writing *Sherlock Holmes vs. Dracula*, sent to me by my copy editor, and was indispensable during the process of revision and later when I wrote *Dr. Jekyll and Mr. Holmes*. I still keep that tattered copy at my elbow when I'm writing a new Holmes story. But you don't need to be a pasticheur to find it valuable, as well as a diverting read when nothing else on your shelves seems to fit your mood.

Tracy, Jack, with Jim Berkey. *Subcutaneously, My Dear Watson: Sherlock Holmes and the Cocaine Habit*. Bloomington, IN: James A. Rock, 1978.

This slim paperback, out of print for many years, wastes not a word in examining Holmes's grim addiction, the drug itself, its importance to the detective's life and work, and the harrowing consequences were he to continue in the practice. Much has been written about this side of his life, but this book eschews fulsome speculation in favor of cold hard facts. It's horrendous and riveting.

ACKNOWLEDGMENTS

Thanks go to Jon Lellenberg, veteran editor, Sherlockian, and member of the board of directors that oversees the Conan Doyle Estate, for his part in bringing most of the stories in this book to the public for the first time, and for permission to use the characters created by Sir Arthur Conan Doyle.

The thing would not be possible but for the genius of Sir Arthur Conan Doyle, whose works still shine, and are found in every well-stocked library on earth. The inscription on his headstone, taken from his knighthood epic, *The White Company*, applies to him yet:

BLADE STRAIGHT

STEEL TRUE